REACH WITH ALL YOUR HEART

MARILYN CRAM DONAHUE

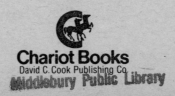

Chariot Books
David C. Cook Publishing Co.

A Quick Fox Book

Published by Chariot Books,
an imprint of David C. Cook Publishing Co.

David C. Cook Publishing Co., Elgin, Illinois 60120
David C. Cook Publishing Co., Weston, Ontario

REACH WITH ALL YOUR HEART
© 1980 by Marilyn Cram Donahue

Cover design and illustration by Kerne Erickson

Fourth Printing, 1988

Printed in the United States of America

93 92 91 90 89 88 1 2 3 4 5

Library of Congress Cataloging-in-Publication Data

Donahue, Marilyn Cram.
   [To catch a golden ring]
   Reach with all your heart / Marilyn Cram Donahue.
     p. cm.—(A Quick fox book)
   Previously published as: To catch a golden ring.
   Summary: Thirteen-year-old Angie is upset when she
hears another girl call the street where she lives a slum,
then feels responsible when her best friend loses his legs in
an accident while trying to escape from it.
   ISBN 1-55513-755-5
   [1. City and town life—Fiction. 2. Physically
handicapped—Fiction. 3. Los Angeles (Calif.)—Fiction.
4. Christian life—Fiction.] I. Title.
PZ7.D71475Re 1988   [Fic]—dc19   88-14807
                                 CIP
                                 AC

ACKNOWLEDGMENTS

My special thanks to my dear friend Carol Reader, R.N., and to Joan Keller, R.N., rehabilitation coordinator (both of San Bernardino Community Hospital) for the generous sharing of their time and for their invaluable technical information.

To Trini
Who walks tall today

Contents

1
BUNDY STREET

Angie skated hard. She was going too fast on the rutted sidewalk, but she didn't care. It felt good to go fast. The cool air rushed past her, twisting her straight brown hair into long tangles and drying the sweat inside her elbows and behind her ears.

It had been hot and horrible inside the roller rink. It was the first day of summer vacation, and everybody was supposed to be celebrating. But she was glad she had left. Angie squinted hard and wiped the back of one hand across her eyes. She let the noise of the six o'clock traffic and the steady whirring of her urethane skate wheels fill her head, so that everything in her mind was a dull roar.

Bundy Street was next. She was almost home. "Angie! Wait for me."

She heard Con's voice, but she didn't slow down.

Traitor! He'd stood right there and let stupid Jessica tell everybody at the skating party that Bundy Street was a . . .

Angie could feel her face growing hot all over again. She wished she could remember all the things she had told Jessica. Whatever they were, she was glad she'd said them.

"Angie! What's the matter with you?"

Con was right behind her, but Angie didn't turn her head. She coasted past Pete's Parking Lot, dodged Old Lu's flower cart on the corner, and skidded to a stop when the light turned red. She made a hard left turn and had already started down Bundy Street when she felt Con's hand on her arm.

Angie was tall for thirteen, and slim, like all the Raffertys. She was also strong, especially when she was mad. But Con was bigger and stronger. He reached out and whirled her around in a half circle until she was facing the other way; then he stopped her short, right beside the little tree that the city had planted in front of the Oak Apartments.

"What are you trying to prove? You could break your neck skating like that!"

"I was in a hurry." Angie spoke the next words very slowly, through her teeth. "I still am."

"Look, Angie. You don't have to be mad at me. I'm not the one who said we live in a slum."

She put both hands over her ears. "Don't say that word to me. It's a lie. Why didn't you stand up and call Jessica a liar?"

Con raised both eyebrows. "You were doing a

10

pretty good job of that. Anyway, it doesn't do any good to start an argument with someone like Jessica. She likes to put people down. All the others know it."

Angie shook her head. "Bundy Street is where we live. Nobody should call it Slumsville."

Con put his hands in his pockets and looked down the length of the street. "It's where we live all right." Then he lifted one shoulder and let it drop in a shrug. "I guess we're used to it."

"What do you mean by that?"

She hated it when people said only half of what they were thinking. Con did it all the time. He was her best friend. She liked him better than anybody she knew, but sometimes she couldn't figure him out.

He was staring down the street. The skin between his eyebrows made a deep question mark.

She looked down the length of the street, too, trying to figure out what he was seeing. Everything looked just the same as it always did. She closed her eyes and sniffed. It smelled the same, too. When you stood at this end of the street, you could always get a whiff of the popcorn from the Mayan Theater.

The 6:15 bus sprayed the air with exhaust and screamed to a stop at the corner of Bundy and Sixty-third. Then it gave a massive sigh and lurched forward like a large, red monster. Angie could see the yellow sign that extended across the back and boasted in black letters: BEAUTIFUL MUSIC . . . KLMN.

11

A siren whooped, pounding the air with a steady beat, and car horns played a staccato rhythm against the low roar of engines. From two doors down came the unmistakable smell of hot pastrami and the sound of Tony Genovese's hand organ. Tony ran the Deli seven days a week, but on Saturday night he took his monkey to Chinatown and played for pennies. Tony Genovese was one of the last of the hurdy-gurdy men.

Angie smiled. People like Tony didn't live in slums.

She nudged Con. "What's eating you, anyway?"

He turned and looked at her. For a second, the sunlight was on his face, and she could count the freckles. Angie's little sister, Caro, had freckles, too, but that was natural, because Caro was a redhead. Con's hair was the color of wet beach sand, but he still had thousands of freckles.

"Nothing's the matter," he told her. "It's just that . . . I guess when you look at the same things every day, you really don't see them any more."

There he went again. Angie's other friends talked about each other. Con was the only person she knew who talked about thoughts. It made her feel uncomfortable, as if somebody was about to pull a rug out from under her.

"Don't be silly," she snapped. "I can tell you anything you want to know about this place, and I look at it every day."

Con shook his head. "That's not what I mean. You look at things, but do you really see them?"

He left the question hanging between them—

like a wet shirt on the clothesline waiting to dry—and turned away, skating slowly along the broken sidewalk.

"I don't know what you're talking about," she said to his back. But she did know. Deep in her throat, she felt a tiny bubble of understanding. She kept swallowing it like a bitter pill, but she had the feeling that it was getting bigger and bigger and that, pretty soon, it would have to come up. She caught up with him and matched her rhythm with his. She didn't intend to talk about it any more.

But Con wasn't through. He skated past Tony's and pointed to the stucco front of the Universal Mission. "Just look at that!"

Angie saw the cracked, yellowed glass set high under the roof in six square windows. In between the windows was a larger-than-life figure of what seemed to be George Washington, covered with gold paint. He was standing on top of a metal frame that held neon letters spelling: PRAYER CHANGES THINGS. In one of the mission windows was a large sign that said Love your country.

Propped against the closed double doors sat a fully clothed sunbather, apparently asleep. Along the front of the mission, pieces of stucco had chipped away and exposed irregular patches of red brick siding.

Angie shrugged. "It looks just like it did yesterday."

"That's right. And I'll bet your eyesight was just as bad then as it is now." Con lowered his voice. "Can't you be honest, Angie? Can't you try to see

13

things the way they really are?"

Angie stared at him until her eyes blurred. Then she knelt quickly and loosened one skate. She took her time pulling the lace up tight, waiting until she didn't have to blink any more.

She knew Con was waiting for her, but she got up slowly and brushed the dusty knee of her jeans. She wasn't going to look at him.

"Hey," he said. "I'm sorry. Listen, Angie . . . I didn't mean to . . ."

Angie looked straight ahead and started to skate. When she felt Con reach for her hand and squeeze it, she didn't pull away, but she didn't look at him either. They passed Corky's, Customer Parking Only, and waited at the corner for the light to change.

Through the tangle of traffic she could see the other side of the street. She knew Con was seeing it, too, but he was keeping his mouth shut. She could hear the music behind her, coming from Corky's. It always started early on Saturday night. But she didn't really listen. Con's words were in her head, louder than when he had spoken them.

Can't you be honest, Angie? Can't you try to see things the way they really are?

Did that mean seeing them with Jessica's eyes? Angie looked across at Chico's Cabin. It was made of logs, painted bright red. Gray barbecue smoke was coming out of a thick chimney on the back side.

Chico himself was standing in the alley, wiping down the outdoor picnic table with the splinters in the top. He cleaned it once a day, he boasted, whether it needed it or not.

Chico's curly hair was thick and bushy, and he tied it back with a piece of white string. His apron looked dirty, but Angie knew it was just stained from the grease. Once, when she had asked him why he didn't buy another one, he had looked at her as if she were crazy.

"This one here has only got two holes," he'd explained.

On the other side of the driveway called Chico's Alley stood Hoang Chou's Laundry. There was a tiny label on the door that said so. But the large black letters across the upper floor—where Hoang Chou lived with his wife, Amy, and eight kids— said West Coast Desk Company.

"Why don't you change the sign?" Angie had asked.

"Free advertisement. All the people who are shopping for desks will find out about my laundry."

"But what about all the ones who are looking for a laundry?"

Hoang Chou had grinned. He had lots of shiny gold teeth. "They can smell that," he'd told her.

It was true. The steamy wet vapor seeped through the walls of the old building. What Hoang Chou didn't know was that it didn't go very far before it smelled like the rest of the street: a deep city fragrance. A mixture of hot tortillas, barbecue smoke, popcorn, pastrami, dusty asphalt, exhaust fumes, and carnations from Old Lu's cart.

The old green building where Angie and Con lived was next. It had one front door, like ordinary houses, but inside it was divided up the middle by a narrow stairway, which stretched like an open accordion to the second floor. There were four apartments on the bottom, two on each side of the stairs. The second floor was identical.

The eight front steps of the apartment were flanked by four skinny white columns, which had once decorated the side door of Morrison's Funeral Home. Black iron handrails connected to the columns.

The light changed, and Angie skated across the street, feeling the bottom of her feet vibrate from the rough surface. The barbecue smell from Chico's made her stomach growl. She glanced at the picnic table in the alley. It was covered with food scraps and black flies.

Angie supposed Caro was getting hungry by now. "My mother's going to kill me," she told Con.

"Why? You're not late, are you?"

"I . . . didn't tell her I was going." She could feel Con looking at her. "She wouldn't have let me."

They reached the house and clumped noisily up the wooden steps. He put his hand on the doorknob. "I hope it was worth it," he said.

Then he opened the door. The hall was dark and smelled like stale bread. But it wasn't quiet. Inner doors slammed, like echoes behind the walls. A telephone rang, and rang again. Mrs. Marenga, from upstairs, was singing in her low gypsy voice. Water gurgled in the pipes . . . was silent . . . then gurgled again. From Angie's apartment (to the right of the front door) came the sound of broken glass, then muted gunshots and a siren.

Angie bent and unlaced her skates. The broken glass was probably real. The rest was television.

Con already had his skates in his hand. "You still mad at Jessica?"

"Wouldn't you be?"

He shrugged. "She's not worth it. If I'm going to get mad, it has to be over something big."

He grinned and put one finger on the tip of Angie's nose. It was a kind of secret thing between them. It meant "I'm OK ... you're OK." Their signal for a smile.

But Angie didn't feel like smiling.

"Come on, Angie!" He waited.

Lately Con had seemed like more than her best friend. She didn't always understand him, but she would do anything in the world for him. She knew he felt the same way.

Angie smiled.

"That's better. Hey! Do you have to baby-sit?"

"Probably." Her mother worked weekends whenever she could. Tips were good at Corky's on weekends.

"How about popping some popcorn? We could take it up on the roof."

Angie hesitated. "Caro would have to come, too."

"So what? She's a good kid. Anyway, I want to get out tonight."

Angie knew why. Con had a new stepfather. He'd had several, and this was the worst of the bunch. It wasn't because he was out of work most of the time. It was because he was just plain mean.

"Why don't you eat dinner with us?" she asked. She knew her mother wouldn't mind. She liked Con, and Angie was the one who did the cooking anyway. She did a quick calculation. They had fresh wieners, but no buns. Bread would have to do. There were some apples and plenty of powdered milk, and she'd noticed an unopened sack of potato chips that morning.

Con looked relieved. "I thought you'd never ask. Wait a minute. I'll get rid of my skates and be back in a second."

He climbed the stairs two at a time. Angie knew he didn't have to ask permission. His mother wasn't the kind to worry. "Con is fifteen," she would say. "He can take care of himself."

Angie moved toward her own door. Her mother said they were lucky to live at the front of the house. The apartments were larger there, and you could see up and down Bundy Street from the kitchen window.

The door opened before Angie had a chance to turn the key in the lock.

"Where have you been?" Her mother's face looked as tight as Angie's felt when she pulled her hair back hard and fastened it with a rubber band.

"There was a skating party. It's the first day of vacation. I didn't think you'd mind."

That wasn't true. She knew her mother would mind. How could she go to work if Angie wasn't there to take care of Caro?

18

"We have rules in this house, young lady!"

Angie looked at the floor. "I'm sorry if I worried you."

"You didn't!" Her mother was very white. "But you made me late for work. I could lose my job!" She walked past Angie without another word. But at the front door she turned.

"I'm working extra hours, Angie, so we can get out of here someday. Do you want to live on Bundy Street for the rest of your life?" She closed the door quietly behind her, but Angie felt as if she had slammed it hard.

Bundy Street! Bundy Street! Was that all anybody could talk about? Angie waited until she was sure her mother was gone; then she went to the front door, opened it, and stepped out onto the bright green porch.

The sun was setting, and the western sky was streaked with crimson cloud trails. For a few seconds Bundy Street was a pink reflection. Angie had seen it at sunset a hundred times, but today she made herself look at it hard.

Old Lu was pushing her flower cart across the street. Nobody knew where she went at night. She just disappeared until morning.

A few lights blinked on in the Oak Apartments, but most of the windows were as dark as closed eyes.

The Deli was a dark spot between the brightness of the Mayan Theater and the flashing neon sign of the mission.

Corky's parking was already full, and there was

a gang standing on the corner listening to free music. She couldn't see Chico's, but she knew he would be closing. He said it was a rough corner after dark.

This was Bundy Street. This was where she lived.

The sun's rays turned to silver and bounced like well-aimed flashlight beams off the corrugated metal lids of Saturday's trash cans, still lining the sidewalks. Then the light faded. The sky turned gray. The street was full of moving shadows.

This was the way it really was.

2

CAROUSEL

The roof was like a big flat porch, sitting on top of
the house. It was surfaced with black tar paper and
edged with a low stucco wall. It was Angie's favorite place on a clear night.

A salty summer breeze blew in from the ocean
seven miles away and swept the air clean. If Angie
wanted to, she could lie on her back like Con and
pick out the constellations that they'd learned
about in school. But what she really liked to do was
lean against the top of the wall and watch the city
lights. From here she could see for miles.

That's the way it had always been. But not tonight.

"What are you so mad about?" Caro stuffed a
handful of popcorn into her mouth and stared at
Angie, waiting for an answer. Con rolled over on
his stomach and reached for an apple.

"She's not mad. She's just thinking."

"About what?"

"About living here."

"Oh . . . What's there to think about? It's a dump. As soon as I get old enough, I'm leaving."

Angie had to hand it to Caro. She was only ten years old, but she faced facts.

Angie came away from the wall and plopped down on one of the big pillows that they'd found in the closet of the empty room on the third floor.

"How old do you think is old enough?" Angie asked.

Caro wiped salted butter off her mouth with the back of her hand; then she brushed her hand off on the seat of her jeans.

"As old as you are," Caro said. "Three years to go for me."

Angie didn't know why anyone had to baby-sit Caro. She had been making her own plans since she was five.

"Look at it this way," Caro explained. "If you don't get out of here while you can, you never will. You'll be trapped, like mom. I'll bet she'd run, if she could. But she's got us."

Caro reached for an apple and took a bite. "I don't know what's keeping you two." She looked at Con. "Especially you."

He reached over and pulled her red hair. "Running away isn't always the answer. Haven't you ever heard of the truant officer?"

"Hah!" Caro made a face. "Haven't you ever heard of staying out of sight?" She got up and took the rest of the popcorn with her. "I'm going downstairs to watch television. It's getting cold up here."

Angie nodded. "Go ahead. We'll be right down." She put one elbow into her pillow and twisted so she could look at the sky. If she had wings, she'd just take off. Fly as high as she could and look for a better nest. But she wasn't a bird. Birds didn't live on Bundy Street.

Con stood up so suddenly he looked like he had been pulled up by a string through the top of his head. Other people unfolded themselves, but not Con. He always went straight up.

"How can you do that?" Angie asked him.

"Leg muscles. From swimming, I guess." He laughed. "I haven't got wings, Angie, but I can go almost anywhere on these legs."

It was probably true. Con was a real athlete. He could run and jump and swim like nobody she'd ever seen. He had only started high school this year, and the coach was already talking about varsity teams.

He stretched his arms high, as if he was reaching for the crescent moon that hung between two stars. "If I could fly, that's where I'd go. I'd hang from the moon and swing like a monkey."

"But you can't fly, Con. Nothing flies around here. Not even real-for-sure flies. Look at the ones at Chico's. They just crawl around the top of the table and buzz." Angie suddenly felt heavy, as if she weighed one thousand pounds. "It's all your fault," she said.

Con looked surprised. "I'm to blame for Chico's flies?"

"You know what I mean. You told me to take a good look at Bundy Street. Well, I did, and I wish I hadn't. I felt better when I was mad at Jessica."

"Come on, Angie. Pretty soon you're going to sound like Caro."

"She's not so dumb."

"She's not so smart, either. She talks big to hide the way she really feels. Look, if you ran away, where would you go?"

"Someplace where I could get a job." Angie shivered. It was getting cold out here.

"At thirteen? You're nuts."

He was right, but she wasn't going to say so. She stood up. "I have to check on Caro."

"No you don't. You just want to change the subject."

She wasn't going to listen. She went to an opening at the edge of the roof, turned around backwards, and climbed down the metal ladder that led to a narrow balcony at the back of the house. Then she opened the door into the empty room on the third floor. She tossed the pillows into a corner and kept right on going. Her feet beat a syncopated rhythm on the steps, and her fingers barely skimmed the railing.

Con was right behind her. He was still talking. "Look, Angie, just because you face facts, you don't have to let the truth get you down."

She looked over her shoulder. "What do you expect me to do? Celebrate?"

He shook his head. "You have to have a plan. You can stand almost anything if you have a plan."

Angie leaned against the door and waited. "You have all the answers, don't you?"

"Nope. But I've got a few good ideas."

"Such as . . .?"

Con smiled. He had a large freckle right in the corner of his mouth. "Rule number one: When you feel like you're going around in circles, enjoy the ride."

Angie narrowed her eyes. "I think you really are crazy."

"Probably. Can you get out of here by ten tomorrow morning?"

"Maybe. What for?"

"Don't you have any imagination, girl? To enjoy the ride!"

Con took the stairs three at a time and stood at the top, laughing. He knew she couldn't stand a secret. Angie opened her apartment door and slammed it shut behind her.

"Enjoy your own ride," she muttered. But she knew she would be ready by ten. Wherever he was going, she wasn't going to be left behind.

She was ready before ten. She slipped early into the tiny kitchen off the living room and stirred some powdered milk into a glass of water. The toaster was broken again, so she lit the gas burner with a match, standing way back and stretching out her hand. Last week it had caught with a whoosh, and had taken the hairs right off her right arm. Then she stuck a long-handled fork into a piece of bread and toasted it over the open fire.

She had to move like a cat. This place was so small and old, one squeak would wake everybody. She and Caro slept together in a bed that dropped down out of the living room wall and folded back up again like an ironing board. At one time a painted panel of wood had covered the bottom of the bed so that in the daytime it looked like a bookcase—if you didn't stand too close. But the panel had split from the weight of the bed, and now there was just a flowered curtain, gathered on two rods that stretched across the top and bottom of the springs and kept them from showing.

Angie thought her mother had been pretty clever to think of that. But Jessica had taken one look and called it tacky. Angie often wondered what Jessica's house looked like. Big, probably, with more than one bathroom, and a stove that lit when you turned the knob. No beds in the living room, and lots of grass in the yard.

Angie sighed and chewed her toast. She put her glass in the sink and tiptoed back into the living room and through the door into the narrow hall that led to the bathroom on the left and her mother's room on the right.

She washed her face with cold water, because the hot faucet made a grinding noise. Then she stood outside her mother's door, trying to breathe without making any noise. Her clothes were in there. There was only one closet in the house.

She opened the door and listened. Steady, even breathing. She took six steps across the room. Opened the closet door. Found clean jeans and a T-shirt.

"What do you think you're doing?"

Angie dropped everything. Her mother was sitting up in bed, watching her. Her eyes were blinking rapidly, as if she couldn't decide if she was asleep or awake.

"You scared me to death!" her mother exclaimed. "What are you looking for?"

"My clothes." Angie might as well tell the truth. "Con wants me to go somewhere."

"Where?"

"He won't tell. It's a surprise."

"Well, go on. Just let me sleep."

"What about Caro?"

Her mother moaned. "If you wake her, she's yours."

"Don't worry, I won't. Hey . . . mom?"

"What is it?"

"I was going to leave you a note."

"Sure you were!" Her mother sighed and sat up again. "OK, OK, I believe you. Have a good time." She fell back against the pillow. "Angie . . .?"

"Yeah?"

"Try to be home by four? I'll fix dinner tonight. But I really can't be late for work again."

"Sure, mom."

Angie pulled on her clothes and walked carefully across the living room. Caro turned over and groaned. Too much popcorn. Served her right.

Angie smiled to herself. They weren't too bad, her family. Better than Con's. She ran outside to wait on the front steps.

When Con wasn't there, she leaned against one of the pillars and scuffed at a stray weed with her shoe. She'd noticed it a few days ago, growing right out of a crack in the concrete and climbing up the side of the steps like a vine.

She heard voices from upstairs, left front. That was Con's apartment. His stepfather was talking loud, but the words jumbled, and Angie couldn't make out what he was saying. She could hear Con, though.

"This place is crowded, all right. It was full before, but now it's crowded!"

Then the window slammed, and she couldn't hear any more. Poor Con. It must be awful to have a stepfather who yelled at you all the time.

Angie's own father had left when Caro was a baby. He had to go away. Their mother said so, and then she wouldn't talk about it anymore.

Angie tried and tried, but she couldn't remember what he looked like. She liked to pretend that he had just gone away for a while, like the father in *Little Women*. He might walk in the front door any day. She knew the way it would be; she had rehearsed the scene a thousand times in her mind.

He would be singing as he came down the street. He'd have a huge voice, like Tony Genovese's.

He would stop singing and whistle a little as he came up the steps. Angie could see the shape of him clearly in her mind. He'd hold the black railing in one hand. His head would be high, and under his arm would be a long box—red roses for her mother.

He'd have something for Angie, too. In his pocket, in a blue velvet jeweler's box with a snap-top lid. It would be a golden ring with miniature flowers carved into its surface and Angie's full name—Angelina—etched in tiny, delicate letters.

Angie would be the only one home when he arrived. That was the way she imagined it. She would walk to the door and stand there with her heart beating hard and sweat on the insides of her hands.

Then she would reach out and turn the knob. The door would open, and she'd hold out her arms. She'd feel herself lifted in the air, way up off the worn flowered carpet, and swung round and round until she was dizzy.

She would feel the strength of her father's arms and the roughness of his brown jacket. She would smell the lotion he used after he shaved. She'd hear his deep voice saying over and over, "Angie! Angie!"

But no matter how hard she tried, she never saw his face.

"Angie! What's the matter with you?"

Angie blinked rapidly. It was Con. "I . . . guess I was daydreaming."

"You sure were. You were a million miles away."

His voice was hoarse. Angie looked at his face and wondered what had happened upstairs.

"Well, I'm back now," she said. "Where's this

ride we're supposed to enjoy?"

"Patience is a virtue," he told her.

Con took her by the hand and started off at a run down Bundy Street. They arrived at Chico's corner just before the number 15 bus did. It stopped with a shriek of brakes and paused just long enough for Con to pull Angie on behind him and drop his coins in the slot. Then it jolted, hissed, and inched forward as the light turned green.

"We're going on a *bus* ride?"

"Temporarily. Then we have to walk."

That was evidently all he was going to tell her. Angie sat back and looked out the window. She'd never been on the number 15 bus. The sign in the window said La Mirada. That would mean La Mirada Beach. She'd been to the ocean a few times, but not to La Mirada.

What was so special about La Mirada Beach? Maybe they were going for a boat ride. She nudged Con. "I get seasick," she said.

"Then you'd better stay out of boats. Relax, Angie. I'm not telling you a thing until we get there."

It was a long twenty minutes, full of sidewalk scenery and brief, jolting stops. Angie noticed that all the cross streets had numbered names—Fifteenth, Fourteenth, Thirteenth—and the numbers were getting smaller and smaller with every block. When they reached Third Street, Con pulled the cord and stood up.

"This is it. We walk from here."

Angie stepped onto the curb and looked around.

They were at the top of a hill. The sidewalk descended like a curving pathway, past small shops and cottages. A field of television antennas sprouted above the rooftops, reaching up like long rakes to scratch the clouds. Red geraniums, small white daisies, and the crisp blooms of purple everlasting flowers grew in window boxes and in small, sandy flower beds.

They started down the hill. The sun was hot on Angie's back, but a fresh wind cooled her face and blew her long straight hair back out of her eyes. She saw the ocean ahead, deep blue and sprinkled with white foam. Con walked faster, and she had to run a few steps to keep up.

"Where are we going?"

Wherever it was, it couldn't be much farther. They would be walking in the water in a minute.

Con pointed. "Straight ahead."

Straight ahead was the ocean. A large pier rose high off the sand and stretched out across the water. Angie had seen piers before. Most of them were full of fishermen. But this one was different. It looked like an amusement park on the water.

She followed Con up the row of steep cement steps to the surface and looked around. Brightly painted booths were filled with souvenirs: stuffed animals, fancy hats, even goldfish in bowls. Carnival music was punctuated with the *Pop! Pop!* of target guns. Dozens of roller skaters hummed by on their broad urethane wheels. Laughter rose and fell with the sound of the surf.

Con was pulling her by the hand towards a red

ticket booth with a glass top. A golden sunburst covered the front, with sea nymphs dancing in its rays. The corners were lions' heads, and the entire top was like the red-and-gold crown of a king. Painted on the front window was the word *TICK-ETS* in fancy letters.

Con put some coins on the counter and picked up two yellow tickets. "Come on!"

He put both hands on her shoulders and turned her around until she was facing the big round building behind the ticket booth. The sign above the entrance spelled C-A-R-O-U-S-E-L in red letters lined with gold.

The crowd surged forward, and Angie stumbled through the turnstile. The music she had heard outside began again, slowly at first, then faster, until the room was filled with a sound like a thousand hand organs.

She started to speak, but her voice caught in her throat. She'd seen merry-go-rounds in movies, but she'd never been this close to one.

Wide-eyed horses held their heads high. Painted manes tossed wildly. Nostrils flared, and silver hooves pranced to the rhythm of the carousel. Faster and faster . . . round and round . . . up and down.

The whole thing reminded her of a giant music box. If she got on, she would be just like Alice going through the looking glass into another world. She took a quick step backward, but Con caught her by the hand.

"Pick a horse, Angie. This is the only place in the

world where you can go around in circles and enjoy the ride."

As if at his signal, the merry-go-round slowed and stopped. He pulled her to the platform and helped her onto a pink horse with large purple eyes.

Angie's stomach did a quick flop, and she held the brass pole tightly with both hands.. Con climbed onto the horse next to hers. Then he leaned over and pulled her seat belt tight. She wondered what it would feel like when the carousel turned. She hoped she wasn't going to be sick.

"Hey, Angie . . ."

She looked at Con and knew he must have read her mind. He reached over and loosened her fingers. "You don't have to hold on so tight. If you reach out your hand, you might even catch a golden ring."

3

TOOK

Golden ring? Angie shot a question at him with her eyes. He gave her a freckled grin; then he pointed to a contraption attached to the wall of the building. It stuck out like a horizontal metal arm with a shiny silver loop at the tip.

"But that's a silver ring," Angie said.

"It sure is. Only a few are gold. Brass, really. Every time you ride by, you're supposed to lean way out and reach for one. Put your finger right in it and give it a pull. When the music stops, the attendant comes around and collects all of them. If one of yours is gold, you get a free ride."

Angie touched her upper lip with the tip of her tongue. "How far out is way out?"

Con grasped the pole with his left hand, put his weight on the right stirrup, and leaned out as far as he could stretch his right arm.

34

Angie shook her head and held her pole tighter. "I can't do that." She was already feeling funny, and the ride hadn't started yet.

Con stared at her. "I don't get it. Last night you were skating down Bundy Street like a maniac."

"That's different. I knew what I was doing there." She bit her lip. "Are you sure this thing is safe?"

Con got a funny look on his face. It was a kind of smile, but he wasn't laughing at her. It was the way he looked sometimes when she had to ask him to open a jar of peanut butter.

The music started, and she felt her horse quiver. Suddenly, Con unbuckled his belt, slid from his horse, and climbed quickly onto the one in front of Angie. Then he twisted around and looked at her.

"Watch me," he ordered. "Do just what I do."

The platform was really moving now, faster and faster. To Angie's horror her horse was moving, too. Up and down. Up and down. She tried to smile, but her mouth belonged to somebody else. The music filled her head, louder and faster, bells and chimes and organ sounds all mixed together and about to explode under the canopy of bright lights.

Then she looked into the center of the carousel. Panels of long mirrors gleamed like cut glass, echoing the lights and reflecting bright figures as they whirled by like pieces of a kaleidoscope.

Angie caught a glimpse of herself, crouched low over a horse's back. She was huddling. There was no other way to describe it. She had the strange feeling that she was seeing a reflection of the way she felt inside, and she didn't like what she saw. She shifted a little in the saddle and wiped one sweaty palm at a time on her pants. Then she took a deep breath and sat up straighter.

Gradually she felt herself relax with the movement and the music, and daring to hold the brass pole with only one hand, she reached out and ran her other fingers over the enameled surface of her pink horse's head.

In front of her, Con was going up as she went down. The whole carousel was a syncopated dance, choreographed by the flashing mirrors in the center.

Suddenly Con twisted around so he could see her. His eyes lit up. She was glad he hadn't seen her a few minutes before.

"Now, watch me!" he ordered.

He stood, his weight on his right foot, waiting. When they passed the ring machine, he stretched out his arm, hooked a finger into the loop, and pulled. A silver circle came away free, and another popped immediately into its place. It was just like pulling paper cups out of a dispenser.

When they were little, Angie had always boasted that she could do anything he could do. She wasn't so sure about it now.

The next ring came into view. Con took it and waved his hand triumphantly. Two bright silver circles now dangled on his finger.

The carousel turned full circle, and Con claimed a third ring. "Silver again," he complained.

Angie reached for the next one and missed. Her

fingers didn't even touch it. On the next try, she felt a quick brush of metal against her fingertips. She was getting closer. Next time, she leaned as far as she could without falling out of the saddle. She touched the loop, caught it with her index finger, and felt it slip away.

"I don't think your arms are long enough," Con teased.

She didn't even look at him. She was going to make him eat his words. The carousel was still whirling, but she felt a difference, an almost imperceptible slowing of tempo, like music getting tired.

Con reached out in front of her and snapped off a ring. He had a handful now—all silver.

She was right behind him, but there wasn't much time left. She stood all the way up. Her finger was in the loop. She closed her eyes and pulled.

It all happened in an instant. "Look!" she cried to Con. Only when she opened her hand to show him did she realize that the ring she held was gold.

"Beginner's luck!" he exclaimed.

But Angie knew he was as excited as she was. He slipped from his horse and helped her down. His hands stayed around her waist for a second, and he stood smiling down at her.

"Do you want your free ride now?" he asked.

Angie shook her head. "Let's wait awhile. Her legs felt wobbly, like she'd been riding a real horse.

The attendant was working his way towards them, holding out a brown wicker basket that was rapidly filling with silver rings.

"Can I keep mine for a while?" Angie asked him. "We want to come back later."

"Sure. Just show it to the lady at the ticket booth, and she'll let you in. We don't have to worry about people bringing back our gold rings. They all want their free rides."

Angie stuffed it deep into the pocket of her jeans and followed Con through the exit and onto the pier. It smelled different than Bundy Street here. Mostly, it was the salt. It penetrated everything. Even the hamburgers cooking on a hot grill smelled a little of the sea. Angie licked her lips and tasted it on her mouth. The ocean, she decided, had a faraway smell, stretching your mind like a rubber band.

She and Con walked to the railing and leaned against the rusty metal, looking over the side to the water below. It was green, topped with white bubbles and brown seaweed.

"It's a long way down there," Angie said.

"It's a long way *out* there." Con swung his arm across the horizon. "That's where I want to go, Angie. It's a big world, and I want to see what's in it."

Angie felt the gold ring in her pocket. Too bad it wasn't a magic carpet. "You're forgetting something," she said aloud. "You and me, Con, we're stuck on Bundy Street."

Con put his arm around her shoulders, squeezed her hard, and laughed.

"That's only temporary," he told her. "Remember what I told you about having a plan? I'm not going to be on Bundy Street forever, and neither are you. Listen, Angie, Mr. Erickson at school says I have a pretty good chance of getting an athletic scholarship for college. What do you think of that?"

Angie watched his face. It was as if a light bulb had gone on behind his eyes. She was happy for him, but she had a queer feeling inside. She thought it must be the way a person would feel if he missed his plane.

She stared hard at a large pigeon. It hopped along the railing, stretching its iridescent green neck in the sunlight. Angie flapped her hands vigorously. *You can go wherever you want, so go on and go,* she said to herself as she watched the pigeon.

The bird made a single sound, low in its throat, and took to the air.

"Well, what do you think?" Con was asking. "Hey, Angie. What's the matter?"

He leaned over and looked into her face; then he sighed loudly. "You never listen to a thing I say, do you?"

"I'm listening now."

He sighed again. He looked at her, she thought, as if she were not very bright. So what? She didn't feel very bright. Con would get a scholarship and go away. Then she'd probably die, and they'd bury her on Bundy Street. It wouldn't make any difference anyway.

"You're a smart girl, Angie. But sometimes you

can't see what's under your nose. Do you think I'd make a plan that didn't include you? You're a better student than I am anyway. You won't have any trouble getting a scholarship yourself, an academic one at that. Sure, you'll be a year or two behind me, but . . ."

He put out one hand and touched hers. "That just gives me time to pave the road. Look, Angie. Don't you see? School is our ticket out of Bundy Street. I know we can do it—the two of us together. But it has to be our plan, not *mine*."

Angie couldn't look at him. "I thought—" she murmured.

"I know what you thought. You're pretty dumb sometimes." He gave her a gentle poke. "Come on."

They walked past booth after booth, all packed together with common walls, so that the noises and smells from one leaked over into all the others. Hot dogs, hamburgers, pink cotton candy, saltwater taffy—even French fried potatoes in paper containers with catsup dribbled over the top.

The end of the pier was packed with fishermen. Their poles stuck out above the water like long, threaded needles. Every now and then a line would quiver, then tense and pull, as a fish took the bait.

"Look!" said Con. He pointed high in the sky above their heads.

Angie peered into the bright sunlight and saw four long-tailed Japanese kites drifting lazily on the soft air. Suddenly one of them—a red dragon with a purple head—swooped and curled in a long figure eight, encircling a yellow paper butterfly. It was wonderful to watch. Angie took a deep breath and let it out slowly. She wished she could stay here at La Mirada Beach forever.

Then she heard the sound of a boy coughing. She'd heard that cough before. It sounded just like his voice—high and kind of whining. She closed her eyes and hoped she was wrong.

Then she heard him speak. "Hey, Howard, what're you doin' here?"

Con's real name was Howard. Howard Conway. But Angie only knew one person who called him that. Took.

Con looked at Angie, and the name passed, unspoken, between them. Why did Took always have to show up where he wasn't wanted? He was like a black cat, Angie thought. He crossed your path and brought you bad luck.

She turned around and saw him. He had his thumbs hooked into the loops on his pants where a belt should have been. He always stood like that, he always wore a dirty shirt, and he always had a bad cold. Angie didn't know why Con put up with him. He reminded her of a weasel with a runny nose.

"Hey, Howie," Took was saying. "How about some surfing? The waves are good, and a lotta the guys are down there."

He motioned toward the sand on the beach below. His voice was wheedling. He glanced quickly at Angie as if she were a piece of seaweed that he could push away with one foot. Then he began to whine again.

"C'mon, Con. They've got the volleyball nets up."

Angie wondered how much trouble she would get into if she backed him up to the rail and pushed him over into the ocean. She had just about decided it would be worth the risk when Con reached out and thumped Took on the back.

It was a friendly thump, and Con's voice was friendly, too. "Not today, Took. Thanks, anyway."

Angie watched with amazement as she realized what Con was doing. He was turning Took around and starting him off in the opposite direction.

"You go ahead," Con said, "and we'll see you later." He waved his hand. "Can't beat good waves."

"Yeah. Well . . ." Took stood a few seconds, hesitating; then he said, "Too bad ya got obligations." He nodded his head toward Angie and gave Con a wink.

She would have pushed him over right then, but Con had her by the arm. He steered her to an empty bench and sat down. "You shouldn't let Took bother you," he said.

"I can't stand him. He's like a—"

"I know. But he can't help it. It's all a put-on. He tries to act important, because he doesn't have anything to act important about."

Con scooted down on the bench, sitting on his tailbone and leaning his head against the back until he could look at the sky.

"I feel sorry for Took," he said.

Angie shrugged. "Who cares about Took?"

He gave her a quick look. "That's just what I mean. Nobody cares. Took could disappear tomorrow, and he probably wouldn't even become a missing person."

Angie had to agree with that. Privately, she thought that Took's disappearance would be a blessing. She knew she wouldn't miss him.

Con sighed. He did that sometimes when he was about to say something he'd thought a lot about. "Do you know why Took is an outsider, Angie?"

She could think of about a million reasons. She opened her mouth, but Con kept on talking.

"It's because we keep him outside. We don't try to understand what makes him the way he is."

Angie sniffed. She didn't want to understand Took. She didn't even want to talk about him anymore. She dismissed him with one sentence. "He's not my responsibility," she said.

Con stretched his arms over the back of the bench and stared straight over the water. He stayed that way several seconds before he spoke.

"Maybe he's not," he told her. "But don't be too sure. Sometimes we don't get to choose our responsibilities. They just fall into our laps."

Angie looked at him sideways. She wasn't about to ruin this day with an argument, so she kept her mouth shut. But she knew one thing for sure. Never, in her whole life, did she intend to take any responsibility for Took.

4
A PERFECT DAY

The music came so softly at first that Angie wasn't sure she even heard it. Mixed with the roar of the surf, it sounded like bagpipes, far away. It stopped, and hesitated, then began again.

"Tony!" she exclaimed. "What's Tony doing here?"

Tony Genovese, his monkey, and Tony's hurdy-gurdy machine were coming toward them. All the Genoveses had been organ grinders. Hurdy-gurdy men, Tony liked to call them. They used to make their livings with their hand organs and little monkeys; but times had changed, and now the Deli paid Tony's bills. His hand organ was saved for weekends.

It was a beautiful old-timer, made of dark, polished wood and painted with a border of yellow roses. Tony said it had been in his family for more than a hundred years. It reminded Angie of a giant music box, set in a cart on wheels. Tony pushed it wherever he wanted to go, while his monkey, Bandit, rode inside in his own tiny compartment.

Right now Bandit was on the outside, perched on top of the organ, where he could stretch his tiny neck and look around. Tony stopped in the middle of the wharf, dangled Bandit's leather rope in one hand, and began turning the crank with the other.

The music came out, loud and clear. Angie loved it. It was happy music. It made her feel gypsy free. When she listened to Tony, she didn't live on Bundy Street. She was a whisper on the wind.

The sound was a kind of signal to Bandit, too. He wrapped his tail around Tony's arm and swung, landing with a light-footed hop on the ground.

He didn't use a cup. Not this monkey. He picked up the coins with his miniature fingers. He wasn't particular. He'd take them from the ground where they were thrown, or he'd reach into the palm of your hand and let you feel his tiny nails. Angie liked it best when he tipped his hat. It was held on by a strong elastic under his chin so that it always popped right back into place.

Today Bandit wore red-and-white polka-dot pants with a hole in back for his tail and a yellow shirt with gold military buttons down the front. His collar was always the same—a narrow strip of leather with a metal loop that fastened to the rope.

Tony held the rope lightly in one hand and manipulated it with his fingers. One tug . . . two tugs . . . a little jiggle. Bandit seemed to know exactly what he was supposed to do. With the other hand Tony turned the crank of the organ. And with his mouth he made little kissing sounds and spoke soft, meaningless words. Bandit understood those, too, but he didn't always do as he was told.

Angie loved it when Bandit decided to do things his own way. He somersaulted and cavorted, putting pennies under his hat instead of into his pocket. Tony let him do it, laughing with the crowd, and only using the rope to keep Bandit from straying too far away.

"He's a free monkey," Tony liked to say. "The rope is only for communication."

Angie knew it was true. At Tony's house Bandit was really free. Sometimes he got into a lot of trouble, like the time he threw grapes all over the kitchen floor or when he pulled the cat's tail and wouldn't let go. But he never tried to run away. Angie thought he must know how much Tony loved him.

The music stopped, and Bandit sprang to the top of the organ. Tony took a tiny glass from an inside compartment and waited while Bandit drank, and drank again. Then he carefully emptied Bandit's pockets and put the coins in a metal box.

Con waved his hand. "Hey, Tony! What're you doing here?"

Tony gave them a smile. "Chinatown on Saturday nights isn't enough to keep Bandit happy. This summer we decided to tackle La Mirada on Sunday afternoons. So, what've you kids been up to?"

Con laughed. "I'm showing Angie how to go

around in circles and enjoy the ride. Show him, Angie."

Angie reached in her pocket and pulled out the golden ring. "Con says it's just beginner's luck. What do you think, Tony?"

Tony took off the little hat he wore with the yellow feather in the side. "Could be," he said. He wiped his forehead with a bandana handkerchief and put his hat back on. Bandit perched on his shoulder and made soft noises in his ear.

Tony nodded. "Bandit says beginner's luck just means trying harder." He sat down on the bench. "I never argue with Bandit."

Angie put the ring away and leaned back against the bench, letting the sun warm her all the way through. The salt air brushed against her skin, fanning her face and cooling the heat prickles on her arms and legs. It carried with it the distinct odor of corn dogs.

"Mmmm . . ." she murmured.

"You took the words right out of my mouth," said Tony. "Here," reaching into his pocket, "it's my treat."

He handed Con some coins. "Hurry. They only taste good when they're hot."

Con was back in a minute with a cardboard tray loaded with corn dogs, lemonade, and plastic packages of mustard.

Angie wished they could stay like this forever. Sitting in the sun, smelling fish, and eating corn dogs that tasted vaguely of saltwater.

"This is the life," she said.

She felt Tony looking at her. "For a while," he agreed. "Everybody needs to take a break. But then it's time to get back to doing whatever it is you do." He got up and brushed off his pants.

"This organ will get rusty if I don't make it sing." He gave them a nod of his head and began turning the handle. "You kids have a nice time. It's a perfect day for coming to the beach."

His words made Angie feel warm inside, as if the sun had gone right through her skin. Even remembering that she had to be home by four o'clock couldn't ruin this day.

They walked slowly out to the very end of the pier, where the Bait and Tackle Shop hung over the wooden steps that led down to the fishing barges below. Con went to the open window and bought two frozen bananas. The chocolate covering was bitter and good, and it lasted all the way back to the beginning of the pier.

Angie turned to speak to Con and saw him leaning over the railing looking at something below. It was a climbing gymnasium cage, set in the sand beneath the pier. It was quite tall, built on thick stilts that were carved like totem poles with laughing faces. A flat wooden platform with a hole in the middle lay on top of the stilts, and three pyramid-shaped cages rose above the whole thing.

The idea was to shinny up the poles, go through the hole, and work your way up one of the cages to the top. Several children were struggling up the poles.

"Look," he said to Angie. "Do you see who I see?"

Took. He didn't see them, because he was leaning over.

"Look at me!" he shouted to the children. "I'm at the top!"

"Of course he's at the top. He's fifteen years old," Angie exclaimed.

Con shook his head. "For Took, it was probably a hard climb." Then he took Angie by the hand, and they walked to the sidewalk and started the climb to the bus stop at the top of the hill.

Halfway up, Con began to swing Angie's arm—back and forth, back and forth. She thought they must look like two people in a television ad. That was all right. It had been a storybook kind of day. She grinned at him, and they both started to laugh.

They sat by an open window on the bus so they could feel the wind. It was fun, looking out and counting off the streets, with nothing else to do. Sixty-second, Sixty-third . . .

The bus squealed its brakes and pulled to the curb. Angie didn't even remember getting off. But they must have walked along Bundy Street, because the next thing she knew they were at the front steps of the apartment house.

Con opened the door for her; then he reached out his hand and touched her face with his fingertips. "Angie . . ."

She looked up at him and smiled. "It was a perfect day," she said, softly.

"Con!" It was a man's voice. Loud. With a harshness that made them both jump.

Angie looked up to the top of the stairs. Orly,

Con's stepfather, stood, holding onto the rail for balance with both hands. He was a big man, but he seemed larger than ever standing above them like that. The way he looked at them made Angie shiver. She suddenly felt as if she had been caught doing something wrong.

Con didn't look at her. "Go on inside, Angie."

"Oh, Con—"

"Go on, I said!"

She seemed to be moving in slow motion, backing toward her door, fumbling in her pocket for the key. She found it and twisted it in the lock.

"I'm waiting for you, Con." The voice was even louder now.

Angie stood with her back to the door. She seemed to have lost her voice. *Don't go up the stairs, Con. Go anywhere, but not up there. Run!*

Con's face had turned very white, but he didn't run. Angie held her breath as he started climbing the stairs. She watched until he reached the top. Orly smiled at him, then moved back and made a mock bow, sweeping one arm out with the palm spread forward.

"After you," he said.

For such a big man, he had a small smile. It made his lips look tight and reminded Angie of a dog, just when the growl begins, deep in its throat.

She swallowed hard. Why was Orly so angry? Con hadn't done anything wrong, unless . . . Could Orly have found out that Con was hiding some of the money he earned?

Con walked past his stepfather, around the

corner of the landing, and out of sight. Orly stayed there, looking at Angie.

He was still smiling. Then, just as if he had clicked a shutter, the picture changed and his face went hard. He leaned over the banister, and Angie could see the glitter behind his eyes.

"Where've you kids been?" he whispered. "What've you been up to?"

Angie still couldn't speak. She wanted to tell him they hadn't been up to anything. She wanted to beg him not to hurt Con. But she just stood there and stared back at him. She felt like she was staring at a big snake that was deciding whether or not to strike.

Slowly, she reached behind her and felt the doorknob with her hand. She closed her fingers around it. It was hard and firm. It gave her a little courage, and she used it to lift her chin and tighten the trembling in her lips.

Orly caught her defiance. He squeezed the banister so hard that Angie could see his arms begin to shake. Then he let his hands drop, and he gave Angie that same tight-lipped smile that he had given Con.

"I'll get you," he told her. "One of these days, when you're not looking, I'll find a way to get you."

His head was nodding up and down like one of those little carnival dolls that can't stop bobbing. Up and down . . . up and down . . . always smiling . . . even when he turned away and followed Con out of sight.

Angie didn't hesitate. Without another thought

she slipped into the apartment and locked the door behind her. She stood, leaning with her back against it, waiting for her heart to stop thumping.

What had they been up to? Orly could make you feel wicked just by standing there and looking at you.

She wondered what he was saying to Con now. She was sure he was yelling at him, because he always yelled. He threw things, too. Once Orly had thrown an electric iron right through the open upstairs window. It had sailed through the air with its cord dragging behind it and had landed in the top of one of the sidewalk trees.

Caro had seen it happen. She said the cord had hung down from the tree just like a cat's tail with a plug on the end. Orly had leaned out the window and laughed. Then he'd pulled Con to the window and made him look out, too.

"That's what's going to happen to you if you don't do what I tell you," he'd said.

Angie stood, with her back still pressed against the door, and remembered how Caro had told the story.

"He meant it, Angie. He was laughing, but he wasn't being funny."

Angie knew now what Caro had meant. When Orly smiled, it was a kind of danger signal. Angie closed her eyes and saw Orly standing at the top of the stairs, bowing to Con. She saw him wagging his head and saying, "I'll get you. One of these days . . ." But she was safe behind a locked door, while Con was . . .

Oh, be careful, Con. Give him your money if he wants it. Just be careful.

Even as Angie thought the words, she had a nagging feeling, almost like a fluttering pain in the top of her stomach, that being careful wasn't going to be enough.

5
SOLITAIRE

"Hey, Angie. Where have you been?"

Caro was sitting at the card table that they used for eating. She had taken off the square of yellow and white oilcloth and was shuffling a deck of cards. A portable fan rotated slowly back and forth, stirring the air in the stuffy room.

Caro didn't wait for an answer. "Want to play double solitaire?" she asked.

Angie looked at her suspiciously. The table was littered with cola cans and potato chip crumbs. An apple core was on the floor next to Caro's sandals.

"Where's mom?" Angie asked.

"Gone to work. She got called in early—a couple of hours ago."

"Oh, boy!" Angie glanced at the clock. It was only a few minutes after four, so she wasn't late.

But she knew her mother hated leaving Caro alone.

"Don't worry," Caro went on. "She wasn't mad. But she said you'd have to cook dinner after all." She shrugged. "I'm not hungry."

"You will be by dinner time." Angie started to walk past Caro into the kitchen, but a loud noise stopped her. A noise like a piece of furniture falling and breaking its sides.

Caro's head jerked up. When she spoke, her voice was too loud and too fast. "Mom said if anything happened, you were to stay inside. She said you were to turn on the television loud and lock the door." She grabbed Angie's arm. "Mom really meant it, because . . . Orly's been looking for Con all afternoon."

Angie didn't stay inside. She unlocked the door and ran out into the hall.

"Angie, don't!"

She turned her head and looked back at Caro. Caro's face was white, and she was shaking all over. "If . . . he gets you, Angie . . . then he'll get me, too. You can't tell what Orly will do."

Angie sat down hard on the stairs. Her legs were trembling. She was shaking almost as hard as Caro was.

But Con, how was she going to help Con? Her throat tightened until she could hardly breathe. It wasn't right to sit on the stairs and listen while someone you loved was . . .

A loud shout from the apartment above made her jump. It was Con's voice, and it was followed by a low moan. That was Con's voice, too. Angie put her hands over her ears, but she couldn't stop the sounds. The apartment door flew open—she could hear it bang against the inside wall—and then the voices were louder than ever.

"That's only a sample!" Orly yelled. "When I get through with you, you won't go fooling around at the beach. You won't be able to go anywhere!"

"What are you trying to prove?" Con's voice was strained, as if he didn't have any breath behind his words.

"I'm the boss around here. That's what I'm proving. From now on things are gonna go my way." There was a terrible crash, then several heavy thuds, like something was being banged against the wall, and the sound of struggling, as if Con was trying to push Orly away. Angie could feel the vibrations right through the stairs of the old house. She got up slowly and held on to the railing. She could hear Caro making whimpering noises at the bottom of the stairs, and she could hear Orly's voice coming from the top.

"Look at me, boy! You're gonna quit school and go to work full time. . . . And all the money comes to me from now on."

"That's not fair—" Con began.

But Orly didn't even listen. He just kept on yelling. "The second thing you're gonna do is stay away from that girl."

"Angie?" Con's voice was low, and surprised sounding.

"Yeah, Angie."

"Listen, Orly. Leave . . . Angie out of this." Con's words were slow and forced as if he could hardly talk. "You can't stop me from being with Angie."

"Oh, can't I? You just try me and see. You like that girl, don't you? You wouldn't want to see her hurt, would you?"

Angie started backing slowly toward their apartment door. Orly meant what he'd said. He would get her. She didn't know how, but she was sure he would think of a way.

The upstairs door slammed shut, and she couldn't hear their voices anymore. She pushed Caro ahead of her into the apartment, and they stood there looking at each other and waiting.

There was another loud crash from upstairs, then another and another. Angie couldn't stand it. "We've got to do something," she said, and was ashamed at the fear that showed in her voice.

"Like what? Call the police?" Caro shook her head. "The minute they arrived, everything would be quiet."

Angie listened. It was already quiet. A door slammed, and heavy footsteps thudded on the stairs. The front screen squeaked and banged back against its hinges.

"Quick!" Angie started for the kitchen window, but Caro was there first.

"It's Orly," she announced. "He's leaving."

Angie didn't wait another second. She unlocked the door and went up the stairs two at a time.

"Con!" she called, pounding on 2A. "Open the door. Are you all right, Con?"

The door opened a crack. It wasn't Con. Bernice looked through the slit. Bernice was Con's mother, and everybody called her by her first name because it was so hard to keep track of her last names. Her face was white, and she had the expression of someone who has been sick for a long time.

"I . . . just wanted to know . . . that is, I heard . . . is . . . Con all right?"

"He'll be all right." Bernice began to close the door.

"Could I see him?"

"No! Go back downstairs. Leave us alone."

Angie had the terrible feeling that if she didn't see Con now she never would. "Please," she said. "Just for a second."

"Go away. If it hadn't been for you, none of this would have happened."

The door slammed. Angie stood in the upstairs hallway for a long minute. At first she stared at the door. 2A. The number was painted in black enamel. The tail of the two had begun to peel.

Something skittered along a crack in the wall and disappeared. Angie knew it was a cockroach, but she didn't bother to swat it. She turned away from the door and went slowly down the stairs.

Con was hurt, and it was her fault. How was it her fault? She went over and over Bernice's words in her mind, trying to digest them by repetition, the same way she tried to learn a hard math problem at school. But math was logical. It finally made sense. Bernice's words didn't make any sense at all.

"Bernice is absolutely crazy!"

Saying the words out loud made Angie feel better. She hadn't done anything bad. She'd gone to the beach, and she'd come home, and she'd stood at the bottom of the stairs, talking to Con.

Maybe that was it. Maybe Orly didn't want anyone taking Con's time. If it hadn't been for Angie, Con might not have wanted to go to the beach and spend the money Orly wanted.

In that case, was she to blame? Was she at fault for just being there?

Caro was waiting in the doorway. "Who are you talking to? Did you see Con?"

Angie ignored the first question and answered the second. "I saw Bernice. She wouldn't let me in. She said Con will be all right."

Caro made a noise like a horse's whinny. "Bernice is stupid. I wouldn't take her word for anything. You ought to go and talk to Tony."

Sometimes Angie could hardly believe that Caro was only ten years old. Of course, Tony was the obvious person to talk to. He was the only one on the block who wasn't afraid of Orly. Bernice would let Tony in, and he wouldn't leave until she had told him the whole truth.

"Look," Angie said, "I'm not going to leave you here alone. We'll both go and wait for Tony."

"Isn't he home?"

"He's at the beach. La Mirada. That's where we went, and we saw him there with Bandit."

Caro's eyes grew round. "You went to the beach?"

"What's the matter with that? We rode the merry-go-round, and we ate lunch and talked with Tony, and we took the bus home. We didn't do anything wrong!"

Caro raised both eyebrows. "Don't yell at me. I never said you did." She waited a minute. "What's it like at the beach?"

Angie looked at her little sister. She thought of Caro staying in the apartment waiting for their mother to wake up. She thought of her walking on Bundy Street, eating by herself at the card table, playing solitaire behind a locked door. Then she thought of the green sea and the air that smelled of salt and the white clouds that moved with the wind.

Feeling guilty about Con was bad enough. She couldn't handle this. "I'll take you there," she said, "and you can see for yourself."

She knew what Caro was thinking. Angie was making one of those "someday" promises that didn't mean a thing. But Angie did mean it.

"Come on." Angie grabbed her by the hand. "Right now we've got to go to Tony's."

There wasn't much traffic on Sunday afternoons. It was easy to jaywalk, dodging two or three cars and a motorcycle that made a queer, choked sound when it honked. Tony's Deli was dark inside, except for the little night light that burned all the time. There was a stone ledge that jutted out beneath the display window. If you put most of your weight on your legs, you could half-stand, half-sit on it.

They didn't have to wait there long. Tony was already climbing off the bus at the corner. It took him a few minutes because of the hurdy-gurdy and because Bandit was sitting on his shoulder hopping and chattering. He looked tired. Angie noticed the slight stoop at the back of his shoulders. When he got closer, she could see the lines around his eyes.

But as soon as he recognized them, he straightened up and smiled. "What a nice surprise. Two beautiful ladies waiting for me. Hey, Angie. What's the matter?"

"Oh, Tony, you've got to come quick. Con's hurt. I know he is. He's upstairs, and Bernice won't let me in." She took a breath. "Orly did it, Tony."

When Angie thought about it afterwards, she couldn't believe Tony had moved that fast. He scooted them back across the street, monkey and all, and stood impatiently while Angie unlocked her apartment door.

"Now, both of you, wait here for me. Take care of Bandit. I'll be back in a little while."

"Wait!" Angie caught him by the arm. "Tony," she whispered, "will you ask Bernice why it's my fault?"

"Your fault?"

She nodded, unable to say any more. He put his hand on her head. "Leave it to Tony," he said. And he ran all the way to the top of the stairs.

The apartment seemed stuffy. Angie turned on the electric fan and sat in front of it. It blew hot air around the room, but it didn't make her feel any cooler. She got up and turned it off and opened the windows instead.

Bandit perched on the edge of the card table and watched her. Every now and then he tugged at his rope, which Caro had tied securely around the table leg. When no one set him free, he opened his little mouth and protested in his shrill, squeaky voice.

Angie knew just how he felt. She wished she could scream like that. Maybe it would make her feel better. If only she were more like Caro! Angie had never been able to sit at the table like that, patiently examining one card after another, putting black on red, red on black. Caro loved to play solitaire.

Angie remembered that she'd seen that word *solitaire* on their dictionary list at school. It meant more than a card game though. It was a word for somebody who lived all alone, like a hermit.

Angie had thought at the time that it was a pretty dumb way to live. It would drive her crazy. But she was alone now, wasn't she? Even in the same room with Caro and Bandit.

She held her head in her hands and shut her eyes. Why was Tony taking such a long time? Could it be because—the thought made her so sick she felt dizzy—Con was . . . dead?

Angie squeezed her eyes tighter. Her mouth was dry, and she couldn't swallow. She really was going crazy. Listen to that pounding in her head. *Thump! Thump! Thump!* No . . . it was the door. Bandit made a terrible racket and began jumping up and down. That meant Tony was back.

For a second she couldn't get out of the chair. She looked across the table just in time to see Caro fumble a shuffle and scatter the deck of cards across the table and onto the floor. Caro started to pick the cards up, then stopped. Her lower lip was trembling.

Angie looked at her sister in surprise. Caro wasn't calm at all. That card game of hers was just a front to hide the way she really felt. Angie pushed back her chair and stood up. She was the oldest here, and it was about time to start acting like it. She went to the door and let Tony in.

"Hush!" he said to Bandit; then he went and sat on the arm of the sofa. Last time Tony was here, he'd found out that the arm was the safest place to sit. Both the two big cushions had broken springs.

Angie stood in front of him, waiting. She thought she would fall down if he didn't say something quick. But he just looked at the floor and shook his head.

Finally Tony turned to her. "Listen, Angie. Con's not all right, but he's going to be all right. Bernice told you the truth about that.

"Bernice is acting a little crazy," he went on. "She wanted to blame someone besides herself, so she picked on you. But it's not your fault, Angie. Not yours, and not Con's."

"Orly?" she asked, once the meaning of Tony's words had registered deep within her mind and reassured her.

"He's gone. If we're lucky, he won't come back.

He wanted Con to turn all the money he made over to him. That's what started all the trouble. He found out that Con had been saving out a little bit each week."

Angie sat up and shook her head. "That's not fair. Con works hard, and Orly doesn't work at all."

"I didn't say it was fair. I said it's the way Orly wants it."

Angie swallowed. Her throat was dry. "Tony, what are we going to do?"

"We're going to eat a late dinner, and then you and Caro are going to bed. Don't expect to see Con for a few days, and don't go upstairs. He'll come down when he feels like it."

Tony got up and headed for the kitchen. "Let's just hope that Orly's gone for good. That will solve a lot of problems."

He opened a can of soup and a box of crackers. "You mix up some powdered milk," he told Angie. "If you want it cold, you'll have to put an ice cube in it."

He heated the soup and poured it into three bowls. Angie wasn't hungry. She didn't intend to eat a thing, but Tony sat there until she did.

Then he stacked the dishes in the sink. "I'm taking Bandit home now," he said. "I want you girls to get some sleep. You did the right thing when you called me." He nodded his head in approval. "I'll check on Con in the morning. Leave it to me."

He closed the door softly behind him, and Angie turned the key in the lock. When she turned around, Caro was pulling the bed out from the wall and would have climbed in it with her clothes on if Angie hadn't stopped her.

"What's the difference?" Caro complained. "I'll just have to put them on again in the morning."

"The difference is that you'll put clean ones on in the morning," Angie said. "There's a right way to do things, and a wrong way."

Caro gave her a funny look. "You make it sound like my whole future depends on whether or not I sleep in my clothes."

Angie climbed into the bed beside her. "I don't know, Caro," she sighed. "Maybe it does."

In a few moments, Caro's breathing was steady and heavy. But Angie didn't go to sleep. She was thinking about what Orly had said. *I'll get you. One of these days when you're not looking, I'll find a way to get you.*

Angie stared at the shadowy ceiling with the plaster cracks that showed even in the dark. She sighed and turned her face to the wall. There was only one answer. She couldn't see Con anymore. The words kept repeating over and over in her head, like a cracked record. Cracked, like the walls around her. Con and she would live in the same apartment building, but they wouldn't be friends. Orly would hurt them both if he saw them together. Especially Con.

Angie used the end of her pillowcase to wipe away the tears. Without Con her life would be just like Caro's card game. She'd play it all alone.

6
A MOONLESS NIGHT

It was late on Wednesday afternoon when Orly returned. Angie was at Second Chance, the secondhand dress store she sometimes worked at, when she looked out the window and saw him coming down the street. A cold shiver started at the back of her neck and made her shudder as if she had seen a snake.

"What's the matter with you?" Flo demanded. She owned the shop and Maria's, the restaurant next door.

When Angie didn't answer, Flo came over to see what she was looking at.

"I was afraid of that," Flo sighed. "Poor Con. Now it's going to be the same old story over and over again. Orly won't let the boy out of his sight. He'll work him to the bone, but he won't lift a finger himself. And that temper!"

Angie picked up a pink sweater and shook it out. Then she put it carefully on a hanger. She was thinking about what had happened the last few days. News traveled fast on Bundy Street. At first everybody was angry about what had happened to Con. There had even been a lot of talk about keeping Orly away. But that's all it was—talk. Here he was back again.

"Do you have anything more for me to do?" Angie asked Flo.

"Not this afternoon. But you can come back in the morning and help in the restaurant. I have to admit it, Angie, I'm always glad when school is out and I don't have to do all the work myself." Flo hesitated. "Say, Angie. Have you seen Con since . . .?"

Angie shook her head. She hadn't seen him at all. She'd been kind of hoping that today . . . or tomorrow . . . Oh, what was the use of hoping? Orly was back.

She went out on the sidewalk and up the steps of their apartment house next door. But she hesitated before she went inside. She was scared of Orly—and she wasn't ashamed to admit it.

"Hey, Angie. Wait up. I gotta talk to you."

For the first time in her life, Angie was glad to see Arnold Tooker. She watched while he stumbled on the bottom step and almost fell.

"Hey, man. There must be a loose board there."

There wasn't, but Angie let it go. She jerked her head toward the screen. "You might as well come in."

She never doubted that Took would go first. He had the manners of a mule. If Orly was waiting inside and hit him on the head, it would serve him right.

She followed him inside and glanced quickly around the hallway. No sign of Orly.

"Well?" she asked. "What do you want?"

Took began to whisper. "Unlock your door, for pete's sake. We can't talk out here."

"Why not?"

Took jerked his head toward the top of the stairs. "You oughta know why not. Orly's back."

Angie unlocked the door, but she didn't like this one bit. "Hurry up," she snapped. "I've got a lot to do."

"Go ahead and do it. I can wait." Took pushed past her and settled himself on the broken springs of the sofa. He squirmed uncomfortably and moved to the padded arm. Then he leaned his head back against the wall and waited.

"Don't do that," Angie ordered. "You'll leave a grease spot."

Took pulled a dirty handkerchief out of his pocket and put it behind his head. Then he closed his eyes.

Angie sighed. Now that he was in, she wasn't going to get rid of him until she heard what he had to say.

"OK, OK. Just make it quick, will you?"

Took smiled. It was a superior smile. She wondered suspiciously what he had up his sleeve.

"It's like this, Angie. I've got a great idea."

Angie groaned loudly.

"Now wait a minute. It really is a good idea. I know how to save Con."

Angie stared at his face. She knew now why Took always reminded her of a weasel. It wasn't so much the way he looked. It was the slyness at the back of his eyes.

"You know how to save Con? That's a laugh, Arnold Tooker. Since when did you ever think of anybody but yourself?"

He didn't answer. He just leaned his head against the wall again and waited. She was stuck with him. He was going to sit there all day.

Angie folded her arms and stood in front of him. "Go ahead and tell me," she said. "But you'd better make it quick."

Took raised his chin. When he stretched his neck like that, he looked like a skinny fish. "I'm gonna take him away from here. I've got a good place for him to go."

"Where?"

Took had his answer ready. Almost too ready, Angie thought.

"To my uncle's place. He lives in Arizona. On a ranch. He needs extra hands." Took paused for effect. "That means he needs extra helpers."

Angie knew what it meant. She stared at him. "Are you telling the truth? Because if you're lying to me—"

"Honest! Why would I lie? Would I be dumb enough to go all the way to Arizona without a place to stay once I got there?"

Angie had to think about it. He was pretty dumb, but even Took couldn't be that stupid.

"Wait a minute. It costs money to go to Arizona. Who's paying?"

"Me and Con will jump a train. Nothin' to it. I've done it before, just for kicks. And we'll leave at night. That way, nobody will miss us for a while."

Nobody will miss you at all, Angie thought.

"And then . . ." Took puffed himself up like he had just won a prize. ". . . then it'll be too late. They'll never find us."

"What's the matter with you? Of course they'll find you. All they have to do is look for you at your uncle's!"

Took blinked rapidly. He did a lot of that when he was nervous. "Yeah. Well, you'll be the only one who knows where we are. I'll . . . uh . . . give you the address."

Angie looked at Took and narrowed her eyes. She looked at him like that until he began twisting his belt flaps. How much was the truth? With Took, it was hard to tell. He acted like a liar all the time. But if any of this was true, it might be a chance for Con to get away from Orly and Bundy Street. His only chance.

"Listen, Took. Why are you telling all this to me?"

He gave her one of those sick grins he was so good at. It wasn't a smile, because he did it all with his upper lip. "You're his girl, ain't ya? C'mon, Angie. Admit it. You'll be the first one to see him when he gets so he can come downstairs. You tell him, Angie. He always listens to you."

Took hesitated; then he shifted his weight uncomfortably on the arm of the couch. He looked as if his clothes had suddenly gotten too tight. "Hey, cut it out, Angie. Quit lookin' at me that way."

Angie didn't answer. She kept on staring until he began to blink and finally had to look at the floor.

"OK! OK! I already told Con about goin' to Arizona—a couple a weeks ago—but he wasn't interested. He said he was goin' to get a scholarship or somethin'. He's crazy, ya know. There's only one way to get out of Bundy Street, and that's to run."

Took was like a piece of cellophane paper, Angie thought. She could see right through him. "Do you have to run from something, Took? Why are you so anxious to get away?"

His face turned red, but he answered her smoothly, as if he had been practicing. "Bundy Street is boring. I'm sick of it. I just need a change, that's all."

Took got up and went to the door. "Con better come with me, Angie. You can tell him. You're the only one he ever listens to." He stuck his chin out defiantly. "Anyway, if you think I'm gonna go up and knock on Orly's door, you're off your rocker!" He paused, his hand on the knob. "Ya just gotta decide whether ya want Con safe in Arizona or dead in Los Angeles. Think about it, Angie."

Her heart skipped a beat, leaving her with the feeling that someone had just punched her in the chest.

Took opened the door to go, but he didn't leave, because Con was standing on the other side, his hand raised, about to knock. Nobody moved. Angie thought they must look like three figures in one of those wax museums she'd read about.

Slowly Con lowered his arm. It was black and blue from his wrist to the hem of his short-sleeved T-shirt. His jaw was swollen, and the skin around both eyes was purple. The bridge of his nose stuck out like a golf ball was caught under the skin. When he started to talk, he looked as if it hurt him to open his mouth.

"What are you doing here?" he asked Took.

"I came by to . . . uh . . . Con, your face is a mess!"

Angie didn't say anything at all. She just stood there and stared at Con. He was standing on his own two feet, and he could talk, but that was about all. He tried to smile at her.

"Oh, Con!" Her voice choked, and she turned away quickly.

In a second, Con was beside her. "Don't, Angie. Come on. Please don't do that." He put his bruised arms awkwardly around her shoulders.

"I'm sorry," she sobbed. "You don't know how sorry I am."

"Hey! You sound like you did it. What's the matter with you?"

"It wouldn't have happened if you hadn't been with me that afternoon."

"Angie, it would have happened if I'd been home all day. Our being at La Mirada just gave him an excuse."

72

An excuse. That's all Orly needed to hurt Con all over again. She couldn't let that happen. Angie glanced quickly toward the door. If Orly knew they were together right now . . . She felt all mixed-up inside. Part of her was so glad to see Con that nothing else mattered. The other part kept remembering what Took had said: *Ya gotta decide whether ya want Con safe in Arizona or dead in Los Angeles. Think about it, Angie.*

"Listen, Con," she began. Then she had to stop a minute. She knew what she had to say. She had decided last night. But it was so hard to make the words come out.

Took cleared his throat. When nobody bothered to look at him, he closed the door and walked over to the couch. He sat down, crossed his arms, and put his head against the wall. Angie didn't want him to be there with them, but she couldn't wait for him to leave. She had to tell Con right now, before she lost her courage.

"Listen, Con. We . . . can't see each other anymore."

Con looked at her a minute, as if he didn't quite understand what she had said. Then his face softened, and he put his hand on her arm. "You're scared, Angie, and I don't blame you. But this isn't the way. Look, I'll get a job like Orly wants me to. That'll keep him happy for a while. No . . . Angie, don't look at me like that. I'm not quitting on you. I'll go back to school someday. Right now I have to figure out how to live with Orly until I can figure out a way to get us both out of here."

Took gave a loud laugh. "You won't last that long, buddy. I mean . . . look at yourself, man. You're gonna get killed hangin' around here."

"That's the chance I have to take." Con tried to smile. It made him look worse than ever.

Took was beginning to sound angry. "Why?" he demanded. "Tell me why you wanta hang around here?"

Con looked at Angie. "I've got my reasons," he said softly.

Angie closed her eyes. "Oh, Con," she whispered. "Those reasons aren't good ones anymore. Orly means what he said. We can't see each other again."

"Cut it out, Angie. There's no point talking like that."

"I'm serious, Con. Orly wants you to stay away from me, and that's what you're going to do. I can't stand seeing you like this. Don't you know that the next time could be worse?" Angie took a deep breath. "Look, I don't trust Took either, but this is a chance for you to get away from here. It may not be the best deal in the world, but it might be the only way. . . . Con, you don't have anything to lose."

"Angie . . . wait. Listen."

"No, Con. You listen." There was only one thing she could say now that might change his mind, and it made her feel like a coward to say it.

"If you decide to stay, Con, we're . . . both going to be losers."

Took stood up. "Hey, that's right, man. Angie

might have her turn. How would ya like to see her lookin' like you look now? Boy, there won't be much left of her when Orly throws *her* against a wall."

Con stared at Took. It was as if he had just realized what Orly's threat really meant. He reached out for Angie with one arm and buried his bruised face in her hair.

When he raised his head, his eyes looked as if he had just opened them after a bad dream—and discovered that things were even worse when he was awake.

"Then there's nothing left for me to do but leave," he said. But he kept holding on to Angie with one arm, as if he never intended to let her go.

"What's the matter? Scared to take a chance?" Took asked, knowing Con needed one final push.

"Take a chance! Don't you think I take a chance just by living in the same house with Orly? I'm afraid all right, but not afraid of taking a chance. I do that every day."

Angie lifted her face close to his. "Then take a chance on staying alive . . . for both of us," she said.

He looked at her for a long minute. Then he put out his free hand and cupped it around the side of her face. Finally, he let both arms drop so that he wasn't touching her anymore. His voice was low and steady when he spoke to Took.

"Were you going to hitch a ride, or what?"

Took gulped, like a fish out of water, then found his voice. "Nah. That's too dangerous. I'm gonna hop a train. It's safe, and it's free."

"When do you want to leave?"

Took's eyes lit up. "Why not tonight? Nothin's keepin' me here."

He was almost dancing, he was so excited. Angie hated him. She knew he didn't want to help Con. He needed him, because Took was too scared to do anything by himself. It made her hate him even more.

But Con was already organizing. "Listen, Took, you wait here while I get some things from upstairs." He hesitated. "Have you got an extra jacket? Orly has mine."

"You can have my poncho," Angie said quickly. It was warm, and she wanted him to have it. She went to the closet and pulled it out. She folded it carefully and handed it to Con.

As soon as the door slammed behind Con, Took began to talk. "Boy, Angie, I'll have to hand it to you. You really knew how to convince him. I owe ya one for that, Angie. I really owe ya one."

"Oh, shut up, Took. Please shut up!"

Took looked surprised, but he closed his mouth and leaned against the wall by the door. His hair was going to leave a grease spot there, too, but Angie didn't even care. She sat on the arm of the sofa and looked at the floor.

In a few moments she heard Con's footsteps. The door opened, and he stood there. He was carrying her poncho, and he had the canvas bag that he usually carried his books in slung over one shoulder.

"Have you got your things?" he asked Took.

Took snorted. "Man, everything I got is on my back."

"Then let's get moving."

Took threw his arm around Con's shoulder. "Right, buddy. You just stick with Took, and everything's goin' to be OK." He gave Angie a wink.

She ignored him and looked at Con, still standing in the doorway. She had seen him like that a hundred times, standing there waiting to come in.

It wasn't too late. She still had time to reach out her hand and pull him into the room. She could tell him she didn't really want him to go. She could keep him here . . . in Los Angeles . . . on Bundy Street.

But she didn't move.

"Thanks for the poncho," he said. His eyes held hers for a long second. When he spoke, his voice was shaking. "I'll be back for you, Angie," he told her. "Someday, I'll be back." Then he stepped backwards into the hallway and pulled the door closed behind him.

She went to the kitchen window and watched as they crossed the street and cut through the corner of Pete's Parking. Con walked tall, she thought. He held his head up, and he walked tall.

Only after she couldn't see him any longer did she begin to cry. She stood in a corner of the kitchen and put her face to the wall. Finally she sank down in a heap on the linoleum.

She didn't know how long she stayed there, but when Caro came over and put her hand on her shoulder, she was sure that her sister knew what had happened. Caro must have been in the kitchen the whole time, standing in the dark listening.

Because she leaned over and said, "It's dark outside, Angie. It's awfully dark. There isn't even a moon."

7

A HOLE IN THE DARKNESS

Angie wasn't asleep. She lay on the bed in the living room and stared into the darkness. It was thick and black. She couldn't find any holes in it at all.

She could hear Caro, lying on her side of the bed, breathing gently. Occasional street sounds came through the walls, but they seemed faded and far away. Her mother had come home quite awhile ago, so Corky's must be closed. That meant it was pretty late.

For a while, Angie had made her mind stay blank. Then, little by little, she allowed herself to think again. Where was Con now? What was he doing? She tried to imagine him sitting on the floor of a boxcar with his knees drawn up under his chin. After a train left Los Angeles, it wasn't long before it reached the town of Indio and open desert. That's probably where Con was now. On the desert. Clattering and swaying, clattering and swaying. Angie had never been on a train, but that's the way she thought it would be.

Would Con ever realize that she'd wanted him to go for his own good? Not just because she was afraid of Orly. It didn't matter, she told herself, as long as he was safe. She thought of the way his bruised face had looked. At least Orly would never do that to him again.

If only he hadn't gone with Took. Took never meant anything but trouble. Angie turned over on her side and shut her eyes. She'd heard it was cool at night in Arizona. She hoped Con was wearing her poncho.

"Angie!"

The sound was like a scratch at the door.

"Angie!"

There it was again. Louder. Urgent.

She sat up in bed and slid her legs over the side. Who in the world would be out in the hallway at this time of night?

Angie felt her way across the dark room and opened the door as quietly as she could. The nightlight in the hallway was bright, and she blinked blindly for a few seconds; then she focused on the figure in front of her.

Took!

Arnold Tooker was standing there staring back at her with eyes that bulged alarmingly. His face was streaked with dirt, and his T-shirt was torn.

One leg of his jeans was hanging open in a loose flap like someone had sliced it with a knife. His skinny chest was going up and down, and his open mouth made a strange, whistling sound every time he took a breath.

He was trying hard to say something. "Your . . . your . . ." Then he began to cough.

Angie pushed past him and looked into the hall. Then she went to the front door and looked outside. Took was alone. Something inside her turned upside down.

"Took!" Her voice was loud as she whirled to face him. "Where's Con?"

Her back was against the apartment house door now, blocking the way. Took stood, half crouching, in front of her. His eyes moved rapidly, like a small animal's. He choked and swallowed. "Your fault . . ." he whispered. "All your fault . . ."

He held his throat with one hand and began to cough again. He tried to speak. His eyes bulged out until she thought they would pop, but nothing came out of his mouth.

Then she saw the poncho. It had been wadded up under Took's arm. He pulled it out—what was left of it—and threw it at her feet. It looked like someone had put it through a meat grinder. She bent to pick it up and saw the stains—felt the sticky wetness that was already drying—stiffening the fabric as if it had been splattered with a dark red starch.

Took was still trying to get his breath, but his voice came out louder now. "Not . . . my fault," he gasped. "Con . . . he wouldn't listen."

Behind him, Angie saw Caro's face in the doorway. Then a light went on in the apartment.

"I knew what to do. . . . I told him. . . . But he . . ." Took's voice rose; then he seemed to choke on his words. He bent over, coughing hard.

Angie grabbed him by the arm and shook him. When he kept on coughing, she shook him again. "Tell me!" she yelled. "What did Con do? What happened to him? Arnold Tooker, you'd better tell me right now, or I'll . . ."

Angie saw her mother. She was pulling a robe around her shoulders and squinting her eyes open as if she were trying hard to wake up. "Angie . . ." she said. "What in the world?"

Took whirled to look at her. Then he began edging toward the door.

"Oh, no, you don't!" Angie stood firmly against the screen, blocking his way. "You're not going anywhere, Arnold Tooker, until you tell us about Con. Where is he? And why aren't you with him?"

Took took a deep breath. He held it so long, Angie thought he would drown in his own air. When he finally let it out, his face changed. It crumpled like a piece of wadded-up paper, ready for the trash. Angie looked at him in astonishment. Took was crying. Out loud. Just like a baby. He was crying and talking at the same time.

"I tried to help him. Ya gotta believe me, Angie. I told him . . . told him to wait . . . to get on a train that . . . wasn't moving. He was in a hurry. That was your fault, Angie. It was your fault he was in a

82

hurry. 'Don't be a fool, Con!' That's what I told him. But he . . . jumped anyway."

Took shuddered. He bent over and held his stomach as if he hurt inside. "I can't stand it," he moaned. "I don't wanta remember."

Angie's mother came over quickly and put her hands on his shoulders. "Listen to me, Took! You have to tell us as fast as you can. What happened to Con, and where is he right now?" She didn't look sleepy anymore, and her voice had a command to it that surprised Angie. Her mother was taking control, just like Tony Genovese would.

Took pointed at Angie. "It was her fault. She gave him the poncho. It was the poncho that caught on the wheels. Con jumped. . . . But it caught and . . . pulled him . . . . Ohhhh!" Took moaned and put both arms around his middle.

"Pulled him where? Took! Listen to me! What happened to Con?" Angie's mother gave him a shake. "Tell me. Right now!"

Took looked at her. "It pulled him under. That's what I've been tellin' ya. We were in the train yards. That poncho of Angie's caught, and it . . . pulled him under . . . under the wheels. Then . . . I came straight here for help."

Took was crying again, but he wasn't making any noise. His face was all screwed up, and his shoulders shook, but no sounds came out.

"Have you told anybody else?" Angie's mother asked.

Took shook his head. She let go of him and ran past Caro into the apartment. In a few seconds,

Angie heard her voice. She was talking on the telephone.

"Operator . . . yes . . . this is an emergency!"

Angie looked down at the ragged poncho. She wanted to push open the screen and run outside. All the way to the train yards. She wanted to find Con. But her legs wouldn't move. The air coming through the screen behind her was cold. She shivered.

The apartment house door was supposed to be closed at night. Closed and locked. No one could get into the hallway without a key. But Took had gotten in. There was only one key he could have used. Con's. And Con always carried it on a metal hook attached to his belt.

She looked at Took. "How did you get in?" she demanded.

"With Con's key," he told her. "I had to use it. How else was I gonna open the door?"

"You're telling me you took time to unhook Con's key from his belt? Then you took time to take off his poncho? And then you took time to come all the way back here?" Her voice was shaking, but she made herself go on. "Took, you don't have any brains at all. You should have called for help!"

Her mother was back now, shaking her head at Angie to stop. "I've just called the police, and the paramedics, too. It isn't very far from here to the train yards, Angie. I'm sure Took didn't waste any time getting here."

Took stretched up his neck. He'd stopped crying, but his face was all red, and he was sniffing loudly.

"Yeah. That's right. I came real fast. And . . . listen, Angie. I didn't waste much time, because he wasn't wearin' the poncho anymore. I picked it up off the ground."

Angie looked at him suspiciously. "And then you left him? Just like that?"

"He . . . didn't care. He didn't know if I was there or not." Took started holding his stomach again. "Con . . . he was makin' a lot of noise. Yellin' and screamin', and . . . I just had to get out of there."

Took sat down abruptly on the hall floor and shut his eyes. "At first, Angie . . . listen . . . ya gotta believe me. I tried to help. But I didn't know what to do."

He squeezed his eyes shut tighter. "I never saw anybody before with . . . his legs almost gone . . ."

"Oh!" Angie's mother clapped both hands over her mouth. When she took them away, they were pressed tightly together in front of her, as if she were praying in church. "Took, look at me. Do you know what you're saying?"

Took didn't open his eyes. But his head moved up and down. "The train got his legs. They were . . . run right over."

Angie's mother turned and started up the stairs. "I have to tell Bernice," she said. "I don't want any of you to move." She looked directly at Angie. "I mean it!"

Angie didn't move. She held her poncho and looked at Took sitting on the floor. She didn't let herself think about what he'd just said. She didn't even let the words repeat themselves in her mind.

Took was a liar. He'd always been a liar. There wasn't any point in listening.

She could hear her mother talking to Bernice upstairs. A door slammed. Then Orly's voice joined the other two. "If the kid ran away," he said, "he can stay away. You tell him that. He knows what's waiting for him if he tries to come back here."

"You don't understand what's happened." It was Angie's mother talking. "I'm trying to tell you that there's been an accident."

"Listen," Bernice interrupted. "Con has always been able to take care of himself. If he wants to stay out all night, that's his problem."

"Will you listen! The boy's been hurt!"

"Says who?" Orly asked loudly.

"You really don't care, do you?"

"Sure I care. I care about getting some sleep."

The door slammed. Then the only sounds in the building were Angie's mother's footsteps, running across the landing and down the stairs.

Con runs down the stairs every morning. He has good legs. He can run anywhere. Angie narrowed her eyes at Took. He was a dirty liar. She wasn't going to believe him. She wasn't!

From somewhere at the edge of her mind a sound began. At first she thought Mrs. Marenga was awake and singing to her baby. But there wasn't any melody to the sound. It hung on the air, rising and falling like something lost in the night.

That's the way sirens always sound, Angie thought. Lonely and far away. But these sirens weren't far away. They were getting louder.

She saw Took get up off the floor and go to the screen door. Then she saw her mother push right past him. She was wearing jeans and a blue shirt. Her long hair was flying loose, and she was trying to tie it back with Angie's only good scarf.

She turned once in the doorway and looked at Angie. "Somebody needs to go and be with Con. No, Angie," as Angie moved forward. "I think you had better stay here. All three of you should stay right where you are. I'll get Tony to come with me, and I'll telephone as soon as I find out . . . anything." She held out her hand, palm forward, as if to hold Angie where she was. "I promise."

She turned and ran down the steps. Red lights throbbed around her. On—off. On—off. Like some alien heartbeat. For a few seconds, Bundy Street looked like it was on fire. Then two police cars and an ambulance screamed down the length of the block and squealed their tires as they turned hard right at Pete's Parking.

Their sirens trailed behind them like the tail of a comet.

"They're heading for the train yards," Took said.

His voice was a dull knife, cutting painfully into Angie's consciousness. She felt Caro close beside her. She felt Caro's hand in hers.

Took pushed the screen door open and went outside. Angie didn't ask where he was going. He stood for a few minutes at the top of the steps; then he slowly walked away into the darkness. She didn't try to stop him.

After a minute, she opened the door and went

outside herself, pulling Caro by the hand. They stood there on the porch, leaning close together. Finally, the sirens began their steady wailing. They were coming from the train yards this time.

Angie followed the sounds in her mind. Along Sixty-fourth . . . coming closer now. She closed her eyes tightly as the ambulance screamed along Bundy Street. When she opened them, the red lights had disappeared, and she saw, instead, the yellow neon lights of the Universal Mission.

PRAYER CHANGES THINGS.

The words blinked at her out of the darkness like a giant advertisement. She stared hard. Angie had always had serious doubts about that sign. Oh, it wasn't because she didn't believe in God. Everybody on Bundy Street believed in God, and they said his name all the time just to prove it. But she and Con had talked about it, and they had decided that God had better places to spend his time. Besides, most of the people who went to the mission didn't go there to pray. They went there looking for a bowl of soup.

Caro began pulling at her hand. "I'm real cold, Angie. Can we wait inside?"

Angie looked down at her sister. "You go on in. I'll be right there." When Caro hesitated, she gave her a little push. "Go on."

Angie stared at the sign a few more minutes. It looked like someone had cut yellow stencils out of the sky and made little holes in the darkness.

When she went inside, Caro was lying in the bed with the covers pulled up over her nose. Her eyes were shut, but Angie knew she wasn't asleep. She always lay like that when she was upset about something. Angie turned out the light and went over to the card table to sit on a folding chair. It was then that she realized she was still wearing her pajamas.

Angie shook her head slowly back and forth. Things hadn't turned out the way she had planned them at all. Instead of safe in Arizona, Con was . . . She squeezed her eyes shut, but she could still see him in her mind. He was probably in the emergency room at West End General Hospital right this minute.

Angie wrapped her arms tight around her middle and rocked back and forth. The memory of Took's voice filled her head until she thought she would explode.

I never saw anybody before with . . . his legs almost gone . . .

Angie clenched her fists and felt the poncho with her fingers. She was still holding it, tight against her stomach. It was stiff now, where the blood had dried. Con's blood.

Angie shuddered and tasted salt as the tears ran down her face and into her mouth. But she didn't drop the poncho. She held on to it and stared straight ahead into the darkness.

"Let him live," she whispered. "Please. He hasn't done anything wrong. Please let him live. . . . Let him live. Let him live!"

The words came from somewhere so deep inside her that pretty soon she didn't have to say them.

She didn't know how long she sat at the card table. But she knew her arms ached and her mouth was dry. When the phone rang, she was surprised to see that the room was light. The night had passed, and it was morning.

8
WEST SIDE GENERAL

Angie could feel her heart thumping as if someone were beating on a hollow drum inside her chest. She picked up the receiver and pressed it close to her ear.

"Angie! Is that you?"

It was her mother's voice.

I'll telephone as soon as I find out anything. I promise. Her mother had said those words last night. Now it was morning, and it was time to hear the truth. Angie swallowed. Her throat seemed lined with rough sandpaper.

"Angie, what's the matter? Are you there?"

Angie swallowed again, and cleared her throat. "Hello," she whispered. Then, a little louder, "I'm here."

"Listen, Angie. I have good news. Con is alive. He's badly hurt, but he's alive."

Her mother's voice made a sudden hollow sound and stopped. There were muffled noises as if someone was fumbling with the phone. Then she heard Tony's voice. It sounded far away, but she could make out the words.

"It's all right, Evelyn," he said softly. "That's enough for now. We'll tell her the rest later."

Then his voice was louder, speaking into Angie's ear. "Are you there, Angie? This is Tony. Listen, Angie. We'll be home in a few minutes."

Angie's voice cracked. "What are you going to tell me later?"

Tony took a quick breath. She could hear it, because he was talking so close to the phone. "Angie," he said finally, "I can't talk any longer. There are other people here waiting to use this phone. I'm going to bring your mother home right now, and I'll tell you everything when we get there. It's been a long night, Angie. How about making something hot for us to drink?"

There was a tired smile in his voice. She could see exactly how it would look on his face. "OK, Tony." She hung up the phone and stood looking at it a minute before she went into the kitchen.

It was quiet outside. An early morning June fog was drifting in from the ocean, leaving wet footprints on Bundy Street. An occasional car crept over the black asphalt and made shushing sounds with its tires. Angie watched the fog float on the air like gray smoke, blurring the neon sign that blinked above the mission.

Had her prayer changed things? Con was alive,

and that's what she'd asked for, wasn't it? Then why did she have such a bad feeling inside of her?

She reached in the cupboard and took out a can of powdered chocolate drink, pried off the top, and measured some into a small pan. Then she added water almost to the top, lit the fire, and began to stir.

She wondered if she should have made a bargain. Like telling God that she would do something for him if he would do something for her. Could she have thought of anything big enough to do?

Angie watched the little bubbles begin to form around the sides of the pan. The sight of the warm chocolate made her sick at her stomach. She swallowed and looked away.

She could have offered everything. She could have said, "Take my life and make Con all right." But she knew she wouldn't have meant it. Angie really didn't want to die. The thought of it scared her. She would do almost anything for Con, but if she had said that she would die for him, she would have been lying. She hated herself for it, but it was the truth.

Now he was alive. But Angie knew that something terrible was wrong, and she would never know if she could have done anything about it.

She shivered, and went into the bedroom and pulled on her jeans and a heavy sweater. She put her gym socks on underneath her sneakers. But when she went back to the kitchen, she shivered again.

A taxi pulled up in front of the apartment and

stopped. Angie went to the window and saw the car door open. Tony got out; then he reached out his hand to help her mother. Taxis were expensive. She wondered why they hadn't walked. It was only a little over half a mile to the hospital.

Her mother looked up toward the window. Her face was white and the skin seemed stretched tight. She took hold of Tony's arm, and the two of them stood there until the taxi had swished away into the swirling fog. Tony lifted his shoulders once and let them drop. He looked at her mother; then they started slowly toward the house.

Angie went to the stove and turned off the fire. She guessed they had had to take a taxi. They looked as if they could hardly walk. The front door opened and closed, and still she stayed in the kitchen.

Con is alive, she kept telling herself. *Con is alive.*

"Angie . . ." Her mother's voice was a whisper from the other room. Then she was in the doorway, but her voice was still a whisper.

Angie didn't answer. She opened the cupboard and took down three cups. Then she carefully began to pour the hot chocolate. She put the cups on the square metal tray that had been the lid of a fruitcake tin that someone had given Flo for Christmas. Flo hated fruitcake and had presented the whole thing to Angie's mother.

When Angie turned around with the tray in her hands, her mother was right there, watching her. She had one of those fake everything's-all-right smiles on her face.

"That looks good," she said. "Just what we need."

She reached out and took the tray; then she stood back and waited for Angie to go in front of her. Angie didn't have much choice. She went into the living room and sat down at the card table with Tony. She didn't look at either of them. She concentrated, instead, on peeling off the top of a fingernail that had a rough edge.

Nobody said anything for a few minutes. Her mother passed around the chocolate, and they all pretended to taste it. When Tony cleared his throat, her mother jumped, the table wobbled, and the hot chocolate made a dark brown pool around each cup.

Angie went to the kitchen for a dishrag. She could hear them whispering in the other room.

When she came back, she saw Caro with the covers still pulled up around her nose and her eyes shut tight. Angie wished she could crawl back in bed and be ten years old again.

"Tell me," she said. "You might as well tell me the truth."

Her mother looked at Tony. He gave her a nod that said, Go ahead. It's time to tell her.

"You know, Angie," her mother began, "this whole thing has been terrible, but the important part to remember is that Con is still alive." She shook her head. "It's a miracle. I don't know how they saved him." She paused for so long that Angie began to wonder if there was any more.

Then, "The thing is, Angie, he was so badly hurt,

that . . . there were complications. His . . . his . . ."
Her mother said the rest so quickly that it sounded
like one long breath. "Angie, Took told us the
truth. Con's legs were caught under the train.
They were taken almost off."

Angie swallowed. *Almost off.* That didn't mean
entirely. Doctors did wonderful things these days.
You read about them sewing on fingers all the
time.

"So . . . he's really going to be all right?" Angie
asked. She looked at her mother, then at Tony.

It was Tony who finally answered her. He took
both of her hands in his big ones and held them
tightly. "Now listen to me," he said. "Con is going
to live, but he's not all right. He's going to have to
live without his legs."

Angie stared at him. "You said they were almost
off! Almost isn't all the way. The doctors can sew
them on. I know they can." Her voice was getting
louder, shriller. "They have to. Con can't be in
pieces. He needs his legs!"

"The doctors did try, Angie. They tried all night.
They finally had to amputate to save his life."

Amputate? Angie opened her mouth, but she
couldn't say the word. It meant cut off. They had
cut off Con's legs.

"Oh, no! I don't believe you." She stood up
quickly and shook her mother by the arm. "Go
back and tell them to try again." She looked at
Tony. "Please, Tony! They have to keep trying!"

"It's too late," he told her. "Angie, they saved his
life. You have to be thankful for that."

She shook her head. "You don't understand. Con's a runner. He has to have legs to be a runner. What's he going to do without any legs?"

She clenched both fists and held them against her cheeks, pushing until her jaws hurt. "If they don't give Con his legs back, I'll never forgive them! Oh, Tony! Please go back and tell them!"

"I can't, Angie." Tony's voice was rough. "The legs are gone, and you can't put them back. You'd better accept that, or you're not going to be able to help Con at all."

Help Con? How could she help Con? After what she had said to him, he might not want to talk to her.

Her mother shook her head and spoke softly. "Tony, none of this had to happen. The boy had a future."

Tony nodded. "I know. But it's no use thinking that way. It did happen. It's over. We can't bring back yesterday."

Talk, talk! They were sitting there talking, and Con was lying in the hospital all alone. Anger boiled up inside Angie until it reached the top and overflowed. She wanted to reach out and pound something—or someone.

"It was Orly's fault," she exclaimed. Her mother and Tony stopped talking and looked at her. "And ... Took's ... and this whole stupid street's!"

"Wait a minute," said her mother. "I'm not so sure about that. Con had his problems. But none of them made him run away until last night. No, Angie. I think something else happened to Con. He never would have run away . . . unless he thought he had no other choice."

They were both looking at her, as if she knew what had happened. But they didn't say anything.

The anger she had felt turned around and went back inside her and burned a hole in her own stomach.

Her mother reached out and put her arm around Angie. "Don't look that way, honey," she said. "We'd all like to find somebody to blame. But what good would it do? Instead, we'd better start thinking about what's going to happen when Con comes home."

Angie couldn't think about that. She could hardly think at all. Suddenly, she had to get out of there. She pulled away from her mother and walked across the room. She put her hand on the doorknob.

"Angie, wait. Where are you going?"

She didn't know. She didn't care. "To the hospital," she lied.

"Angie, it's too soon. They won't let you see him."

Tony put his hand on her mother's arm. "They might," he said. "They just might."

Angie left. She didn't know if her mother called her again or not, because she didn't listen. She pushed open the front door and stood alone on the porch. But she didn't look at the neon sign across the street. She knew what it said, and she didn't believe it.

She looked, instead, at the stray weed that was still trying to grow up the side of the steps. "It won't do you any good," she said out loud. "If you stick your head up around here, you'll just get it chopped down."

She reached out one foot as if to smash it, then stopped. A tiny, heart-shaped leaf was straining upward, standing erect on its fragile stem. It was walking tall, she thought, just as Con had walked last night. Well, let it try. What was one more weed on Bundy Street?

She went down the steps and stood in the middle of the sidewalk. Sunshine was piercing the fog, slicing through it with long, bright beams. Millions of waterdrops reflected the light. She put her hand up over her eyes and squinted. It was as if someone were standing behind the fog with a dozen spotlights, and focusing them right on Angie.

PRAYER CHANGES THINGS blinked at her once, then faded away. She looked down and began to walk fast, following the path of gray concrete. The fog swirled around her like a cold, wet blanket, covering her, following her. She began to run. A horn honked. Brakes screamed.

"Watch where you're goin', why don't cha?"

The car was so close that Angie could put out her hand and touch it. The driver's face was red. He looked angry and scared at the same time—just the way Angie felt. She jumped out of his way, and the fog swallowed him up, like a large animal swallows a small black bug. If she stood there long enough, would it swallow her, too? She didn't want to die, but disappearing didn't seem so bad.

Angie began walking again. She didn't care which way she went; she just moved through the fog, letting it cover her like Caro's blanket. Maybe the fog would last all day, and she would never have to come out.

But it lifted, just the way it always did in June, scattered by the onshore breezes and warmed by the sun. One minute it was heavy and wet and thick, and a few seconds later it turned to wispy trails, floating like sheer lace, moving aside to make room for dingy buildings and early morning traffic.

When Angie heard the siren, she thought for a minute she was standing on her own porch, and it was last night again. Then she saw the red lights, flashing right in front of her. The white ambulance screamed loudly as it pulled out of the long, curved driveway.

Angie stared across the street at the complex of buildings. They seemed to be growing larger and larger as the fog cleared. A red sign at the end of the drive said EMERGENCY in large square letters. There was no other identification, but Angie knew where she was. She and Con had walked past the back side of West Side General Hospital a hundred times. It was something all the kids did, hoping they would see an ambulance come roaring in, watching for a glimpse of the stretcher. Took called it free entertainment.

Angie shuddered. She would never do anything like that again. She stood at the corner and pushed the traffic button on the side of the lamppost. The green light flicked on almost at once. She wasn't ready for it, and stood there, swallowing, unable to move. It turned to amber, then red. Her fingers were shaking when she pushed it again. She jammed both hands into the pockets of her jeans, and felt her right index finger curl around a loop of hard metal.

She pulled it out and stared at the shiny brass ring. She had forgotten all about it. It was only a memento now. Angie tried to remember how happy they had been that day, how the music had sounded, and how they had laughed as they walked together up the hill. But all she could think of was the look in Con's eyes when she had told him they couldn't see each other again.

Angie blinked her eyes hard. She couldn't see very well right now, but she knew where she was going. When the light changed, she walked quickly across the street.

9
ROOM 202

She stood at the counter for a long time, but nobody seemed to notice her. She wondered if she was supposed to take a number, then sit down and wait. But there weren't any extra chairs.

The small waiting room was full of people. Some of them looked sick, and some of them didn't. Doctors with stethoscopes hanging around their necks appeared and disappeared. Nurses walked back and forth carrying trays and bottles and clipboards. None of them stopped. Only the desk nurse was stationary, and she was typing. Click—click ... click—click. Never looking up.

Angie cleared her throat. "Excuse me."

The woman raised her head. "Did you want something?" She looked at Angie, surprised.

Angie thought that was a stupid question. Why

would anyone come to a place like this if they didn't want something?

"I wonder . . . I mean . . . could you tell me where . . ." Angie stopped and tried again. "There was an accident last night at the train yards," she said.

The nurse's face changed. She suddenly looked like a human being. "I'm afraid you can't see that patient now. But you can go upstairs and see if the desk can tell you anything." She hesitated, and looked at Angie curiously. "Are you family?"

Angie thought quickly. If she said she was a friend, they might decide to send her away.

"I'm his sister," she lied.

The nurse gave her a sympathetic nod. "That must have been your mother and father who were here last night." It was a statement, not a question, and Angie let it go. The nurse was pointing to the open doorway at the side of the room. A long, polished corridor stretched like wet glass, interrupted only by two orderlies and a couple of sandfilled ash cans that seemed to float on its slick surface. Angie wondered if anyone ever slipped and fell down.

"Look, honey, you just go through that door and on to the end of the hall. Turn left. The elevator is around the corner. Go upstairs to the first floor and look for information. Maybe they can tell you how your brother is this morning."

Angie thanked her and started down the long corridor. When she found the elevator, it was open and empty. The panel on the inside wall told her that she was on the lower level. She pushed the number-one button and went slowly up.

The lobby was very quiet. She could look through large glass doors and see a few cars going by on the street outside, but she couldn't hear them. The telephone on the information desk rang. It had a muffled sound, and when a woman in a pink uniform answered it, she spoke so softly that Angie could hardly hear her voice.

She went to the desk and waited. The phone sank soundlessly into its cradle, and the pink lady looked up. "Can I help you?" she whispered.

It gave Angie the creeps. Why was it so quiet? Nobody was sick in here. To her horror, she hiccuped. Loudly.

The woman's eyebrows went up. "Can I help you?" she repeated.

Angie needed to go somewhere and hold her breath and count to ten and drink a glass of water. Instead, she tried to look steadily at the raised eyebrows. "I'd like some information, please."

"The name?"

"Con . . . I mean, Howard. Howard Conway. He's . . . my brother. There was an accident last night. A train . . ." She had to stop and swallow. It didn't help. She hiccuped again.

This time the woman pretended not to notice. "Oh, yes. I know about that. I'm sorry."

"Could . . . could you tell me how he is?" Angie closed her mouth quickly.

The woman picked up the phone and dialed a single number. "Information for Howard Conway," she said. "Yes, I'll wait." Angie held her breath and counted to ten. She tried swallowing rapidly three times. Then she read the badge on the woman's uniform. Pink lady: Miss Morrison.

Miss Morrison began talking into the phone. "I see. Yes, I understand." She smiled at Angie. "Your brother is doing as well as can be expected this morning. That's pretty good news, considering all he's been through."

"Can I see him?"

"I'm afraid not. It's just too soon for visitors. Why don't you go home, dear, and come back tomorrow?"

Home? She wasn't ever going home until she had seen Con. She didn't know how she was going to pull it off, but she knew she wasn't leaving.

"Could you tell me his room number . . . so I won't have to ask when I come back tomorrow?"

Miss Morrison consulted her chart. "Room 202," she said. "One floor up. Then go to the end of the hall."

"Thank you very much." Angie turned and started toward the elevator.

"Just a minute, Miss Conway. That's the wrong way." Miss Morrison pointed firmly to the swinging glass doors at the hospital entrance.

The next hiccup was loud—and painful. Angie silently blessed it. She waved her hand at the drinking fountain next to the elevator doors and held her throat. "I need a drink of water," she said. And hiccuped again.

Miss Morrison smiled and went back to her chart. Angie drank the water slowly. When she'd

had all she could stand, she kept the faucet running and pretended to drink some more. The
elevator door opened, and two nurses came out.
Angie lifted her head and watched as they walked
to the desk. They stood directly in front of Miss
Morrison and began talking to her in low voices.

Angie straightened up and stepped into the
elevator. She pressed her back against the side
wall and pushed close. The doors slid shut; then
she pushed two, and began to move.

202. 202. She kept saying the numbers in her
head. All she had to do was walk to the end of the
hall. She wouldn't ask any questions. She would
walk straight to his room, just as if she knew
exactly where she was going.

The elevator stopped, and Angie got off. There
was a small waiting room with a table, some
magazines, and three chairs at that end of the hall.
There was also a door that said Positively No Ad-
mittance. That made it easy. Angie turned right
and started walking in the only possible direction.
The corridor was long and brightly lit and full of
food carts piled with dirty breakfast trays.

Room 232 was first on her left. She could smell
the flowers clear out in the hallway. She glanced in
and saw them, displayed on the two dressers and
by the window—masses of blooms, tied with satin
ribbons. It was more than Old Lu had on her whole
cart.

222 . . . 220 . . . 218 . . . Angie checked the room
numbers off one by one. She felt as if she were
moving on a conveyor belt. Someone had pushed

106

the on switch, and nothing could stop her until she reached the end of the line.

But something did stop her. It was a voice that came from the nurses' station halfway down the hall. "Just a minute! Where are you going?"

The voice belonged to a large, dark-haired woman who wore a cap with two black bands and held a pencil in one hand as if she were carrying a weapon. She stuck the pencil behind one ear and glared at Angie.

"Well?"

Angie pointed toward the end of the hall. "Room 202. I'm going to see my . . . brother."

The nurse frowned and consulted her charts. "Not without special permission, you're not. The only one in that room young enough to be your brother would be 202A, and he just came back from surgery. You would have to be his mother to get in there this soon."

"She . . . that is, our . . . mother couldn't come," Angie said. "That's why I'm here." They didn't have to worry about Bernice, she thought. She wouldn't bother them at all.

"It must have been something pretty important to keep her away at a time like this," the nurse muttered. She shook her head firmly at Angie. "Rules are rules."

Angie looked desperately down the hall. She was so close. She felt like making a run for it. "Oh, please!" she begged. "It's so important. He won't have to talk or anything. I just need to see him. I want to tell him . . ." Her voice broke, and she stopped. It wasn't any of their business what she wanted to tell him.

"What's going on here?"

Angie felt a hand on her shoulder and looked up at a tall, thin man with glasses on a high-bridged nose and a mouthful of large, white teeth. He was wearing something that looked like green pajamas and a flat, green cap that covered the top of his head.

"Now then . . ." He looked expectantly at the nurse.

"This young lady was on her way to room 202, Dr. Stinson. She says she's the young man's sister."

Dr. Stinson patted Angie on the shoulder. "I'm sorry," he said. "Your brother needs all the rest he can get. We just brought him out of the intensive care unit, and it's really too soon for visitors. But come back later. Maybe tomorrow." He gave her another smile. "Why don't you leave your name with the nurse? Then we'll be sure to tell him you were here."

What was the use? She couldn't fight both of them. Angie blinked back the tears and said her name. "Angie. Just tell him Angie was here."

The expression on the doctor's face changed. "You're Angie?"

She nodded.

He took her by the arm and started down the hall, pulling her behind him. "It's all right," he said to the startled nurse. Then, to Angie, "He's been asking for you. Says your name over and over.

He seems to want to tell you something."

Now that she was almost there, Angie wasn't in such a hurry. She pulled back at the doorway. How could she explain that she wanted to stand there for a few seconds and look into the room, to see without being seen?

There were lights in the room, but around the first bed it was darkened, shaded and protected by a large screen and by a gray curtain that slid on rings attached to a metal rod suspended from the ceiling. Con was behind the curtain. She was sure of it.

Dr. Stinson glanced at her, and then stepped into the room and gently pulled the curtain back around the foot of the bed. Con's head was on a pillow. His eyes were closed, and his face was very white. The bruises that Orly had made stood out beneath his freckles like dark blots on spotted paper. His arms were resting on top of the light blanket. They had needles in them, strapped tight with adhesive and connected to long tubes, which were attached to an assortment of bottles that hung upside down from a metal frame.

Angie made herself look at the rest of him. She sucked in her breath and looked away quickly. Where Con's legs should have been was a great, flat emptiness, covered by a blanket.

"Angie . . ."

Con's head moved on the pillow. His eyes stayed shut, but he said her name again. "Angie . . ." His left hand lifted from the blanket, hung in the air a second, then fell.

"I'm here, Con. It's me . . . Angie." She didn't remember going through the doorway. She was only aware of standing close to the bed and watching his face.

"Con . . ." She said his name again.

His eyelids fluttered and opened. He frowned, trying to focus. "Angie?" He opened his hand, reaching his fingers toward the railing that stretched like a fence along the side of his bed.

She put one hand through the slats and touched him. He closed his fingers around hers. "I'm sorry, Angie. I really messed things up."

She had to wait a minute before she could speak. She made herself breathe slowly. In—out. In—out. The taste of salt was strong on her lips. She took her free hand and wiped it across her eyes.

"It was my fault, Con. I told you to go. I was so afraid. I thought something . . . terrible would happen to you if you stayed."

He pressed her fingers. "Not your fault. I . . . know . . . what you were trying . . . to do."

He was so quiet, she thought he had gone to sleep. Just as she started to move her hand away, he opened his eyes and held on tight.

"Took?" he asked.

"He wasn't hurt."

Con nodded. "Good. I . . . tried to get him out of the way. He didn't see . . . the train until it was . . ." He closed his eyes and turned his head away.

Angie felt her jaw tighten. Took had lied. He hadn't tried to save Con at all. It was the other way around. If she didn't do anything else for the rest of her life, she was going to see that Arnold Tooker got what he deserved.

"Angie?"

"Yes, Con. What is it?" Whatever he wanted, she would do it for him. She'd do anything he asked.

"My foot hurts, Angie. The right one. It's really bad. It's kind of like I've got a cramp in it. Would you . . . rub it for me?"

She stared in horror at the bottom of the bed. Con didn't know! They hadn't told him!

He opened his eyes and looked at her. "What's the matter? Angie, what's wrong?"

The doctor's hand was on her arm. His voice was loud and too cheerful. "Visiting hours are over. Sorry, young lady. Time's up!"

He pulled her gently but firmly away from the side of the bed and stood like a large green shadow in her place. "Let's try to get a little rest," he said to Con. His right hand moved to a round red button at the head of the bed and pushed it twice. "I'll give you something for the pain," he promised.

Angie could see Con's fingers tightening around the rails. He was trying to sit up. "What's the matter?" he cried. "I can't move my legs!"

A nurse rushed past Angie and pulled the gray curtain around the bed so that it was like a large tent with Angie on the outside.

"Con . . ." she whispered. "Oh, Con!"

Then she backed out into the hallway and tried not to listen to the low, soothing voices that spoke to Con, telling him over and over that everything was going to be all right.

"No . . . no . . ." he moaned. And then she didn't hear his voice at all.

She stood in the hall until the doctor came out. He put his arm around her. "He really thought his foot was hurting, Angie. It's something we call phantom pain. But don't worry. He's asleep now, and we'll keep him that way the rest of the day. Come back tomorrow. Come as often as you can. The boy is going to need all the family support he can get."

Angie nodded. But she didn't answer. She was hearing Con's voice asking, "What's wrong, Angie? What's the matter?" and the other voices—strangers' voices—telling him, "Never mind, son. Everything's going to be all right."

Lies! They were telling him lies. This whole thing started out as a giant, Took-type lie.

She looked up at the brass-plated numbers above the door. 202. The zero gleamed at her like an empty eye. Or a ring. A shiny, golden ring. That was a lie, too. A promise that never happened.

Angie turned and walked slowly down the hall. She took the elevator down to the first floor, ignored Miss Morrison at the desk, and pushed open one of the glass doors. The sun was shining outside. Horns were honking. Everything about the busy street was the same as it was every day. She felt like lifting up her hand and shaking her fist at God.

I don't know what you think you're doing, she wanted to say. *Why don't you make bad things happen to bad people?*

Angie waited. Probably now she would be struck down dead right in front of the hospital. But nothing happened. She began walking along the sidewalk. Thoughts boiled up inside her as if they had been heating for a long time.

What do you want of me, anyway? she demanded. *Do you want me to believe that big sign over the mission? Well, I don't. I can pray all day for Con to get better, but I know darned well that only tadpoles grow legs!*

Angie suddenly felt very tired. She didn't know what to do. She didn't even know what she was supposed to do.

She dug down into her jeans for the brass ring. When the light wasn't shining on it, it was nothing but a dull piece of metal. That was how she felt. Dull. Like all the light had gone out of her.

She stopped at the first wire trash container on the sidewalk, and stood, turning the ring over and over in her fingers, trying to remember the way she and Con had felt that day at the beach. Then they were winners, and the whole world was theirs. Quickly she dropped the ring into the trash. It slipped into a paper cup and lay there, like a large round eye staring at her. Angie hesitated. She shouldn't have done that. Maybe Con would have wanted her to keep it. She started to reach into the basket.

"Step back there! Watch out!"

Angie jumped out of the way as the large white truck from the sanitation department roared to a stop beside her.

"There's nothin' in there that'll do you any good," a rough voice laughed.

The man picked up the basket and dumped it quickly into the hungry scoop; then he held on to the side of the truck as it rolled away.

Angie took a deep breath and let it out slowly. She stood and stared into the empty trash basket. It looked just the way she felt. Empty.

"I don't know what to do," she whispered. "I need somebody to show me . . ." She squeezed her eyes shut tight. ". . . to show me which way to go."

She waited. For a few seconds she wasn't even sure where she was. She only knew she had to stand there because she had lost her way, and she was waiting for directions.

But nothing happened. No answers dropped out of the sky.

She pushed the traffic button at the corner and crossed the street when the light changed. She walked slowly. There wasn't any place for her to go now but back to Bundy Street. She knew the way there all by herself.

10
CARO

The newspapers called it a tragic accident. Near fatal, they said. A miracle that the boy had lived. The boy's parents could not be reached for comment.

The boy's parents could not be reached at all! Orly was gone, and Bernice with him. Angie had a lot of things she wanted to say to them, but now they were gone. She supposed it didn't really matter; they wouldn't have listened to her anyway.

Tony said that most of the neighborhood had watched them leave. They had started coming downstairs in the morning, while Angie was still at the hospital. They had seemed to be in a big hurry, piling boxes on the sidewalk and leaving a trail of junk along the way. Nobody tried to stop them. Nobody asked them where they were going. Bernice stood alone, by the street, while Orly went and rented a broken-down truck. When they finally drove away, everybody stood out on the sidewalk and watched. But nobody said good-bye.

"Good riddance!" Tony said instead. "We're all better off without them!"

Took had disappeared, too. He hadn't been seen since he'd opened the door and gone down the front steps last night.

It figured, Angie thought. It was just like Took to run away and hide. Last night she had wanted him to find a dark creepy hole where he could starve to death and be eaten by rats. This morning, she didn't even care.

Now it was eleven o'clock in the morning, and she didn't know what to do. She couldn't go back to the hospital until tomorrow. And there wasn't anyone she could talk to here. Her mother had gone back to bed, exhausted. Tony had had to go across the street and open the Deli. All the other people on Bundy Street were talking to each other about the accident.

All but Caro. She was sitting alone in the apartment, playing solitaire. Angie supposed she should get out the broom and sweep around her. But there didn't seem to be any point in cleaning house this morning.

Instead, she went up the stairs to apartment 2A. The door was open. Angie stood there a moment and looked in at the empty room where Con had lived. She couldn't get it out of her mind that Orly might still be here, behind a door, around a corner, waiting in a closed closet. When she went in, she walked softly, as if someone were asleep.

Old newspapers were scattered on the floor. In a corner of the living room was a pile of garbage that was already covered with so many cockroaches that it looked alive. Angie opened the kitchen door and closed it quickly. It was even worse in there.

Under the window that faced the street was a pile of clothing. It wasn't folded or anything—just tossed in a scrambled heap. Orly and Bernice evidently didn't want to be bothered with Con's clothes any more than they wanted to be bothered with Con.

Angie wondered what they'd done with the rest of his things. She remembered the canvas bag that he had carried over one shoulder last night. No telling who had it now.

The only other thing left in the room was a card table with a wide crack down the middle. An empty bottle lay on its side on top of the table where it had spilled its contents all over a scattered deck of cards. They lay faceup—facedown—curled and twisted.

Angie knew they were Orly's cards. Con said that was all Orly did when he was home: sit at the cracked table with his bottle and a deck of cards. He only stopped when he felt like starting a fight.

Suddenly Angie felt a little sick. That was what Caro was doing, wasn't it? Shuffling and dealing. Shuffling and dealing. It was enough to drive a person crazy just to watch her. Angie left the door of 2A standing open and went down the stairs.

She opened her own door and looked at Caro's

startled face. She looked like somebody who had been caught sleepwalking. Angie felt a sinking feeling in her stomach. Solitaire wasn't a game with Caro anymore. It was the way she lived.

"Come on," Angie urged. "I . . . uh . . . I need you to help me."

She went to the kitchen and came back with a pile of empty grocery sacks. Her mother used them for garbage, but she wouldn't miss a few.

"Come on, I said!"

Caro put down her cards reluctantly. "Where are you going?"

"Upstairs." Angie jerked her head in the direction of Con's apartment.

Caro shook her head and picked up the cards. She carefully stacked them and began to shuffle. "I don't want to go up there."

Angie was beginning to get impatient. "What's the matter with you? You can't sit in here all the time like . . . a crazy person and play with little pieces of paper!"

Caro looked up, surprised. "I like it better in here," she said.

Angie knew what Caro was thinking. It was safe in here. It was like crawling into bed and pulling the covers over your head. If you stayed there long enough, you might even forget about the things that happened outside.

Angie didn't blame Caro. But she wasn't going to let her get away with it. She had to figure some way of getting her out of that chair.

"Listen, Caro. Con's apartment is empty. You

don't have to worry about Orly, because I was just up there, and he's really gone."

Caro looked at her sideways.

"I'm telling the truth," Angie insisted.

Caro shrugged and started shuffling the cards. They weren't all facing the same way, but she didn't pay any attention. Angie had never seen her like this before.

"Listen, Caro. I saw Con this morning." That was something Angie had been going to keep to herself. She swallowed and went on. "I got to talk to him. And he talked to me."

Caro looked surprised. "Can he talk?"

"Well, sure he can talk. There's nothing the matter with his voice!"

Caro put down her cards and watched Angie doubtfully. "When is he going to come home?"

"I don't know. That's why I want you to help me. We need to get his things out of the apartment. He can't go back there."

She knew Caro would understand what she meant. This whole side of Bundy Street was owned by a big company in Los Angeles. Whenever anybody missed a month's rent, a man in a black suit appeared at the door. Con's apartment wouldn't be empty long. Angie was sure of that.

Caro nodded. She was beginning to look interested. She had that wise owl expression that she always wore when she was trying to figure something out.

"Well, come on then. This is all we need." Angie waved the grocery bags and opened the door. Caro was still sitting in the chair. "Look, Caro," she snapped, "you either want to help Con, or you don't!"

Angie went out in the hallway and started up the stairs. Before she was halfway up, she heard Caro behind her. Together they went through the rooms, looking for anything of Con's that might have been left behind. There wasn't much. Just the pile of clothes and his schoolbooks. He must have packed the rest in the missing canvas bag.

When they had finished, they closed the door of 2A and stood uncertainly in the hall.

"Where's Con going to live now?" Caro asked.

"I . . . don't know." For the first time, Angie realized that Con didn't have a home. He hadn't had much before, but at least it was an address.

"Could he live with us?"

Angie didn't know that, either. What would her mother say? Mentally she rearranged the furniture to make room for Con. Would he be in a wheelchair? Probably. But he couldn't sleep in it. How would he get on the couch every night? How would he get up in the morning? How would he get dressed? Or take a bath? She didn't know the answers, and she didn't know who she could ask.

"Let's worry about one thing at a time," she told Caro. "We have to find someplace to put these things where Orly will never find them." Angie was sure that it just hadn't occurred to Orly yet that he could sell Con's clothes and books and pocket the money.

They both thought of it at the same time. The

room at the top of the house! Nobody went there unless they were passing through on their way to the roof.

They hurried up the stairs and opened the door. Someone had left the window open, because warm air was blowing in from over the top of Bundy Street, lifting the faded blue curtain and filling it out like an inflated balloon.

There was the usual pile of boxes in one corner, but now they were stacked neatly, several feet away from the wall, leaving a large space behind.

Angie walked cautiously across the room and looked behind the boxes. No one was here now, but someone sure had been. A small candle stood upright on a chipped blue saucer. A can of bug spray stood against the wall. Two pillows were stacked neatly, one on top of the other. On top of the pillows was a dog-eared sports magazine. On the cover was a picture of a young man in a track suit with a number across his chest. The caption was KEEP RUNNING! Then she saw the sleeping bag in the corner.

She moved closer so she could see it better. Con had saved for a long time to buy that sleeping bag. She was with him when he had picked it out.

Caro recognized it, too. She put the sacks she was carrying against the wall. "I'll bet Con moved up here after that fight with Orly," she said. "I'm glad he was sleeping up here. Now he has a place to come back to. It's perfect, Angie. He can live up here, and we can take care of him."

Angie smiled, but she didn't answer. She

watched Caro as she busily took the clothes out of the sacks, folded them neatly, and separated them into piles. Angie didn't help her. And she didn't have the heart to tell Caro she was wrong.

Caro hadn't been at the hospital. She hadn't seen Con. She hadn't stood in the doorway of his room and looked at the empty space at the bottom of his bed.

They would have to find someplace else for Con to stay. You had to have legs to climb to the top of the stairs.

"There!" Caro said, brushing her hands together and standing back to look at what she'd done. She glanced up at Angie expectantly. "Where are we going now?"

Angie stared at her in amazement. Was this the same Caro who had sat at the card table a little while ago? What had made her change?

Suddenly Angie remembered something Con had said once. *You have to have a plan. You can stand almost anything if you know you have a plan.* Well, Angie didn't have any plan at all. But she must have made Caro think she knew what she was doing. Caro was looking up at her now, waiting.

Angie went and took her by the hand. She might not have a plan, but Caro wasn't going to know it. As far as Caro was concerned, they were doing everything on purpose.

Before they reached the bottom of the stairs, Angie knew exactly what they were going to do next.

11
SECOND CHANCE

Flo looked surprised when she saw them standing in the doorway of Second Chance. She was waiting on a customer, and she still had flour on her arms from rolling tortillas. Flo did all the cooking next door at Maria's, and the clothes at Second Chance always smelled a little like hot tamales.

She had taken out part of the wall between the shops so that she could walk through. The connecting door was open now, and Angie looked in. Lunch hour seemed to be over.

It was always packed in there by quarter to twelve. Some people came all the way from downtown for one of Flo's hot tamales. By one o'clock everybody had gone back to work.

The only thing left in the room now was the daily mess the customers always left behind them. Angie went into the little kitchen and came back with a tray, a damp rag, and a bottle of spray cleanser. She handed the rag and the bottle to Caro and began stacking dirty dishes on the tray.

"You can wipe off the tables and the chairs," she said. "I'll wash the dishes. Then we have to sweep the floor."

Flo always made it seem good to work at her place. She poked her head through the doorway for a second and flapped both hands at them. "Thank goodness for you girls!" she exclaimed. "I was beginning to think I'd have to close both stores just so I could wash the dirty dishes! Caro, honey, would you water those plants against the wall? And Angie . . . that crowd drank all the coffee. How about getting another pot started?"

Angie knew what Flo was doing. She never allowed anybody to touch those plants, and she always made the coffee herself.

Caro put the broom behind the kitchen door and did as she was told. She was bustling around, Angie thought, as if she owned the place. Angie stacked the last dish to drain and measured the coffee carefully. She had watched Flo a hundred times. It had to be done just so.

"It smells good," said Caro behind her. "It makes me think of bacon and eggs."

"Did you eat breakfast?" Angie demanded.

Caro shook her head.

"Neither did I!" Angie had forgotten that Flo had ears like a fox. She could hear right through walls.

She appeared suddenly in the doorway. "Lunchtime!" she announced. "You girls shouldn't let me go so long without food. My knees are starting to shake."

Flo could make sandwiches faster than anyone Angie knew. In a few minutes they all were sitting together at one of the clean tables. Angie looked skeptically at the tuna on wheat bread, potato chips, and a large, fat pickle. It was usually her favorite lunch. How could she sit here and enjoy it when Con was . . . like he was?

"What's the matter?" asked Flo. "Something wrong with your lunch?"

"Oh, no, Flo! It's fine. I'm . . . just not hungry right now."

Flo took a large bite, chewed, and swallowed; then she leaned one elbow on the table and wagged her finger in Angie's face.

"Did you see what I just did?"

Angie nodded.

"OK. Now you pick up your sandwich and do the same thing. I know exactly what you're thinking, Angie Rafferty, and I can tell you right now that you're not helping anybody if you starve yourself to death!"

Flo's finger stopped wagging and swooped down to point at Angie's plate. It stayed there until Angie picked up the sandwich and took a bite.

OK, thought Angie. *But it will come right back up again.*

She was surprised when it didn't. Her stomach gave a little lurch and accepted it. She was even more surprised to find that she could take another bite and swallow that, too.

Flo went to the kitchen and came back with a cup of coffee for herself and two cups that were mostly milk for Angie and Caro.

"You're not old enough for black coffee," Flo had told them years ago, and she had never changed her mind.

"Well?" she said, leaning back in her chair.

Angie didn't have to ask what Flo was talking about. Flo was a person who faced facts, and she would want to know the truth about Con.

Angie didn't say anything. She had tucked Con away in a corner of her mind, just the way she did when she got a bad grade in school. As long as she didn't talk about it, it didn't seem real—at least not until the report card came.

Angie knew from experience what happened when you started talking about a thing. It came right out in the open where everybody could look at it and turn it over and poke it to pieces. You could never tuck it away again and pretend it wasn't real.

She felt Flo's hand on her arm. "Angie," Flo said gently. "What has happened, has happened. It's a fact. We have to talk about it."

Angie shook her head. It was one thing to tell Caro that she'd seen Con. It was another to have to remember his room and the empty bottom of his bed.

But there was no stopping Flo when she made her mind up to do something for your own good. "Listen to me," she ordered. "If you hide something bad away in your mind, it grows. Did you know that? It gets bigger and bigger until you feel like it's choking you. The only way you can cut it down to size is to tell somebody about it.

"It's like putting a period at the end of a sentence," Flo explained. "That's how we keep things from getting so complicated we can't understand them. What you have to do right now, Angie Rafferty, is to put a period on yesterday. This is today—Thursday afternoon. Wednesday was over a long time ago."

Angie thought she'd lived a hundred years since Wednesday, when she'd looked out the window of Second Chance and seen Orly walking down the street.

But it seemed like only a second ago that she'd walked down the hall of the hospital to Con's room. She said the only truth she could think of.

"It's so dark in Con's room."

Flo looked surprised. "Angie, have you been to the hospital?"

"It's so dark in there," she said again. "There aren't any flowers." Suddenly it seemed so unfair. "Other people have flowers, but Con only has the shades pulled down and the lights turned off . . . and . . . an old gray sheet pulled around his bed."

Flo looked at her a minute. Then she cleared her throat as if she'd found her voice all of a sudden. "Sometimes people can rest better in the dark, Angie. But you're right. We don't want Con to stay in the dark any longer than he has to."

She got up and fished around in a cupboard. In a minute she came back with a small bud vase made of pink and orange carnival glass. She tipped it sideways so they could see its narrow throat.

"One flower is all it will hold," she said.

Caro sounded disappointed. "Only one?"

Flo set the vase in the middle of the table and put both hands on her hips. "What's the matter with one flower? Bouquets are nice, but they're so crowded you can only see the colors. Ask Old Lu if you don't believe me. She's got a whole cart full of colors, and she knows that one single flower is best of all. You don't get confused by leaves and stems and mixed-up smells."

Caro wiggled in her chair. "What do you do when it dies?"

Flo sighed. "You go out and get a new one." She leaned over and looked at them hard. "Do you girls know what I'm talking about? One flower a day. One step at a time. Give Con something to look forward to every day, because he's not going to get better overnight."

Angie nodded slowly. Flo took all the confusion out of things. She made you think that you really knew what you were doing. It wouldn't be so hard going to the hospital tomorrow if she took a flower with her. She could tell Con about not getting confused, about only thinking of one day at a time. It was a little like having a plan. Angie had never had a plan of her own before.

Suddenly Flo clapped her hand to her head as if she'd just remembered something. "That boy, Angie! He was here early this morning. He came slipping in here the minute I opened up."

That boy? An old, horrible feeling started to fill Angie, seeping through the pores of her skin like a bad taste. "You mean Took?"

"Honey, I don't know his name."

"Took, Arnold Tooker. He's the one who ran away with Con last night. I hate him!"

Flo thought it over. "Well, I suppose it was Took. He was real jumpy and looked like he was about to be sick. He left something here, and said you would know what to do with it."

Flo went to the other room and came back with a canvas bag. It was Con's, and Angie could see by the bulges that it was still full.

"Where is Took now?" she asked. "Where did he go?"

"Beats me. He slipped out as fast as he slipped in. What was Con doing with a boy like that anyway?"

"Took said he had an uncle in Arizona who needed help on a ranch. He asked Con to jump a train with him."

Flo was looking at her with one eyebrow raised. "Con had better sense than that."

"I know. . . . I'm the one who convinced him to go." She avoided looking at Flo and kept on talking, trying to say it as fast as she could. "I was afraid Orly would hurt him again, and . . . and I was afraid he would hurt me, too. I talked him into it. I made him believe there wasn't any reason to stay." Angie's voice stopped working right. She shut her mouth and put her jaws together tight. She had to look down at the table.

"Say, now!" Flo reached out and put her hand

under Angie's chin. "You're not blaming yourself, are you? Listen here! What's done is done. You were trying to help. I might have done the same thing myself. Orly probably would have hurt Con again . . . and you, too."

Flo got up and began clearing the table. "If the two of you are through being useful around here, why don't you scoot out and have a look at Old Lu's flowers. I'll say this for them, they're fresher than Old Lu!"

Flo wasn't being unkind. She was trying to make Angie smile. Old Lu's flower cart was kind of a joke around the neighborhood. The blossoms really were pretty, and they were fresh, too. It was just that they didn't seem to go with Old Lu. She had worn the same clothes for as long as anyone could remember; her skin looked like the outside of a peach that had sat in the sun too long; and she always smelled like garlic, because she chewed it for whatever seemed to ail her.

Flo got up and went to the cash drawer at the back counter and took out a few bills. "Here's your pay for this morning." She looked at Caro, as if measuring her up and down. Finally, she nodded. "You're a good worker, too," she said. "You can come back every day with Angie, if you want to."

Angie stared at Flo. Every day! She had never come every day before. Only when she had needed some money.

Flo must have read her mind, for she looked at Angie and nodded her head vigorously up and down. "That's what I said. Every day. You girls are growing up. If you want a job, you have to be dependable, and that means every day. Ten o'clock. On the dot. That way you can watch Second Chance while I handle the kitchen. Then you can stay and help me clean up after lunch. That leaves afternoons free for hospital visits. Well, what do you think?"

"Thanks, Flo. Thanks a lot."

Flo didn't answer. She began fishing around in her pocket for a handkerchief. She blew her nose hard; then she wiped the corners of her eyes.

"Smog," she said. "It's really bad today."

"Yeah," said Angie. "I know." She picked up Con's canvas bag and put it under her arm. "See you tomorrow."

Flo waved her hand, but she didn't answer. She was busy brushing some sandwich crumbs off of the table.

The girls walked past Second Chance on their way to Old Lu's cart. "I think I'm going to like working in there best of all," said Caro.

Angie nodded, but she didn't answer. She was thinking of all the things Flo had said: about putting a period on yesterday, and living one step at a time, and being dependable. It almost made her think that there might really be a second chance.

She felt the canvas bag over her shoulder and thought briefly of Took. He had disappeared again, and nobody cared enough to look for him.

She didn't care, either. She hoped he stayed away. Took was one person who didn't deserve a second chance.

12
THE WHEELS THAT TURN

The next afternoon, Angie bought a fresh flower from Old Lu's cart and put it in the vase that Flo had loaned her. She was walking along Bundy Street, on her way to the hospital, when she saw Chico. He was leaning against the log wall of his cabin, watching the traffic go by.

"Hi, kid!" he said. Chico called everybody kid. He seemed to have a problem remembering names. "That was . . . uh . . . tough luck about the boy. Always liked him. Glad his old man's gone, though."

Angie nodded. "Me, too."

"You goin' to see him?"

She nodded again. "I'm on my way."

"Well, listen. Tell him . . . to hang in there—and that Chico's thinkin' about him."

"I'll tell him."

"Yeah, and you tell him I've got a little cash put away." Chico scratched his head. "I know the kid won't take charity. You better tell him it's a long-term loan."

Angie didn't know what to say. Chico had a reputation for keeping his money in his own pocket. She didn't think he had ever made an offer like this before.

Chico's face suddenly looked hot, as if he'd been cooking over the barbecue too long. "He's a good kid," he said defensively. "I don't have no family. What am I savin' money for, anyway?"

Angie couldn't tell him the answer to that. But she was so surprised that she thought about Chico, instead of Con's legs, all the way to the hospital.

When she got there, she went straight upstairs. All the way down the long hallway she kept thinking about how she would tell Con what Chico had said. But when she reached the doorway and looked into the room, her knees turned to jelly. She couldn't think of anything but the emptiness at the bottom of the bed.

Con was lying there, flat on his back. His eyes were wide open, staring at the ceiling. He didn't move at all. He didn't even look like he was breathing.

"Con," she whispered. She took a few cautious steps forward. He was so white, and so quiet.

Don't let him be dead. Please don't let him be dead, Angie pleaded silently as she set the flower vase on the nightstand by his bed. Then she reached out and touched the railing that separated her from Con like a fence. Her palms were wet and sticky against the cold metal. She could see the clear liquid that fell one drop at a time from the mouth of a large glass bottle and ran through the length of a plastic tube and into his arm. It didn't seem like enough. Nobody could live on one drop at a time. She reached over and put her fingers over his hand.

"I bought you a flower, and Flo sent this vase," she said.

Con blinked. He closed his eyes and opened them. Then he looked up at the ceiling.

"Oh, Con," she breathed. "You're all right. I'm so glad you're all right!"

She felt his hand tighten into a fist. He turned his head slowly and looked at her. "Sure," he said. "I'm just fine. Couldn't be better!" Then he turned away from her so that she couldn't see anything but the back of his head.

"Con . . . I—I'm sorry. You know I didn't mean it like that. Con, please look at me."

How could she have let herself say such a dumb thing? She took his hand in both of hers and rubbed his skin gently with the side of her thumb. She stood that way a long time. Finally, she began to talk. First, she told him about what Chico had said that morning. Then she told him about working at Flo's and about taking each day one at a time, as Flo had suggested. She told him almost everything she could think of, and still he didn't answer her. There was only one thing she had left out.

"Orly's gone, Con. He took everything with him,

134

except your things. Tony doesn't think he'll be back."

That was when he turned his head towards her. "What about my mother?" he asked quickly.

Angie swallowed. She had forgotten about Bernice. She didn't like her very much. But she supposed Con did. "She . . . went with him, Con. Listen, I'm sure she's worried about you. You know how Orly is. She probably didn't have any choice."

Con shook his head. "She had a choice." He closed his eyes. "I don't feel like talking anymore," he added bitterly.

Angie nodded. "OK, Con."

She stayed a while longer, just watching him breathe—in and out, in and out. Tomorrow would be better, she told herself. Tomorrow Con would be glad he was alive.

But tomorrow was worse. Angie could hear Con's voice the second she stepped off the elevator. "Stay away from me!" he shouted. "I don't need any help from you people. I'm not going to that therapy place. And I'm not going to lie on my stomach, either. What difference does it make if my muscles contract or not? I'm not going to be using them."

Angie ran down the hall and stood, gasping for breath, in the doorway. An orderly and two nurses were standing around Con's bed. What were they trying to do to him? The tubes were out of his arms, and he was propped on one elbow, shaking the other fist in the air.

"C'mon, Con." The orderly's voice was gentle. "You'll really be glad you let us help you. Therapy isn't what you think it is. It's a great place. And it's really important that you start today. C'mon and give it a try."

But none of them moved to touch him. Con looked like he was ready to take on the first one who put out a hand.

A folding wheelchair was open and ready by the side of Con's bed. Angie saw it. Its steel frame was shiny, and the black vinyl seat and back looked like real leather. It was like a whole world opening up inside her head. If they could just get Con into that chair, he would be out of bed and on the move again.

"Con," she said gently, "if you were in the wheelchair, I could push you wherever you wanted to go."

One of the nurses looked at her gratefully and moved over so she could come closer to the bed.

"Big deal!" Con sneered. "Don't you know that I don't want to go anywhere? I just want to be left alone. By everybody!" He glared at them all. But when he looked at Angie, his eyes said: especially by you!

His words were bad enough. But it was the look that made her temper snap.

"You always were bullheaded," she told him. "But now you're worse. You're just plain stupid."

Con glared at her again. "Look who's talking! Nobody with any brains would want to come to a hospital to visit a freak." He took a breath. "You heard me. I'm a freak. . . . Now why don't you get out of here and quit bothering me!"

136

"All right, Con. I'm going. But that doesn't change what I said." Angie was surprised to hear the sound of her own voice. It was low and steady and calm. "You are acting stupid, and . . . you're being mean besides." Her voice dropped to an almost whisper. "You know why I came to see you. You know I'll do anything in the world . . ." She took a deep breath. "But if you don't want to see me . . . I guess I won't be back."

She didn't remember going through the doorway and turning down the hall. She thought she heard Dr. Stinson's voice calling her, but she didn't stop. All the way to the elevator, she kept thinking about the way Con had looked when she'd said those last words. He didn't seem like Con at all. He looked like a frightened stranger who needed something he couldn't find.

She hesitated a second; then she pushed the button. The door clanked open, and she was already inside when someone called, "Wait a minute! Don't shut the door."

Angie pushed the open button and waited. One of the nurses from Con's room appeared. She was out of breath, and held one hand over her chest, as if that would help her get more air.

"He wants you," she said. "I think you'd better come."

Angie nodded and moved out of the elevator to follow her all the way back to Con's room.

The nurse poked her head through the open doorway. "She's here."

The other nurse and the orderly seemed to be

gone, but Dr. Stinson was waiting just inside Con's door. He came out into the hallway and put one hand on Angie's shoulder.

"I think he needs to see you alone, Angie."

The nurse cleared her throat. "Visiting hours are over in fifteen minutes," she warned.

Dr. Stinson didn't pay any attention. "Go on in, Angie," he said gently. "Today we'll make an exception. You can stay as long as you want. The other two patients in Con's room were released this morning. There's nobody in there now but Con."

He paused. "Angie, it's so important for Con to let us help him. He can't just lie there in bed. It's vital for him to start therapy as soon as possible. Maybe you can talk to him."

He gave her a little shove and shut the door quietly behind her. She didn't say a word to Con, just walked over close to the bed. From where she stood, she could see the wheelchair. She couldn't seem to stop seeing it.

Con was staring at the sheets that covered the bottom of his bed. Angie thought she knew what he was thinking. But she didn't speak, and she didn't reach out to touch him. That awful word that Con had said kept rolling around in her mind, blocking out everything else.

Freak, freak, freak.

She was furious with Con for calling himself that. Legs or no legs, she was going to make him apologize. Not to her, but to himself.

Finally he cleared his throat. "Listen, Angie . . ."

She didn't look at him. "I'm listening."

138

"Don't be mad at me, Angie."

"I can't help it. I've never seen you act like that."

"Angie, I'm sorry. It's been a rotten day. I've been feeling ... bad inside. And then they (he waved his hand toward the door) had to come in here and start telling me what to do. Look, Angie, I'd never be mean to you. Not on purpose. . . . You know I didn't mean anything I said."

She turned to face him. Her voice was exasperated. "It's not *me,* you idiot. It's yourself you're being mean to. What are you trying to do? Punish the legs that are gone?"

There. She'd said it. She waited for him to throw her out again. But he didn't. He gave a long sigh and reached for her. She put both arms around him and let him bury his head against her shoulder. She held him there like a baby and stroked his hair over and over again.

"You're the only one who can talk to me, Angie. You're the only one who can make me see myself." His voice cracked, and her blouse grew wet with his tears. "Don't leave me, Angie. I need you. I really do."

She held him there and whispered to him until he began to take long, deep breaths. Then she made her voice come out as calm and sure as she could. "I'm not going to leave you, Con. But that's not enough. You have to do your part. You have to try, Con."

There was a long silence, and she wondered if he had heard her. She bent over to look down at him. "Con . . .?"

His eyes were shut tight, and his face was sad. When he answered her, his voice was muffled, but she could hear his words clearly. "OK, Angie. If it means that much to you, I'll try."

13

MR. ERICKSON

It was a hot summer. It seemed to Angie that it was the hottest she had ever known. Each day she and Caro worked mornings. In the afternoons, Angie bought a single flower from Old Lu to take to Con.

Then Angie would walk along Bundy Street, staying close to the buildings so she could catch a little shade. The heat from the sidewalk came right through the soles of her shoes and made the bottoms of her feet burn.

Every day was the same. In the mornings, people got up early to close their windows and pull their shades against the sun. Then they came outside, where they stood in little groups and drank their morning coffee out of kitchen cups. In the evenings, they stood against their doorways, or walked along the sidewalk. Some of them climbed out on iron fire escapes and dangled their legs in the air until it was almost morning.

This is the way it had been in the summer on Bundy Street for as long as Angie could remember. But this year something else was happening. It was barely perceptible, only a murmur against the sounds of the city. But it was a big change just the same.

Ever since Con's accident, people had started talking to each other. Not just speaking. Really talking. At first they had sounded angry. Angry at Orly. Angry at the train yards. Angry at the doctors who had saved Con's life, but taken his legs. They were even angry at the city government. But after a while that changed.

"Now they're talking to each other, because they found out they like it," Flo said. "Even Old Lu nods her head at everyone. It's almost as if everybody on this street just discovered somebody else lives next door." She shook her head. "Don't count on it lasting, though. Give people a little time, and they always forget."

This time Flo was wrong. People couldn't forget when they saw Angie walking down the street every afternoon carrying one single flower in her hand.

Angie went to the hospital every afternoon and stayed until visiting hours were over and the large, dark-haired nurse with the pencil began making angry noises at her. Sometimes she came back at night, with Tony or her mother or somebody else from Bundy Street.

142

Most of Angie's visits were hard ones. Even after Con started using the wheelchair and going to therapy, no miracles happened. There were times when all she could do was stand there by his bed quietly, while Con closed his eyes and reached for her hand and pretended he was too tired to talk. Then she knew that he had had a bad day. But he needed her, just to be there.

Other times he would open his eyes and look at her, and she felt that he was far away, in some world of his own. Those were the worst times of all. She would reach out and touch him and say his name. And he would look at her with a mist across his eyes, and she knew she had lost him for a little while.

One day, a few weeks after the accident, she had almost reached the end of the hall when she heard voices coming out of Con's room. A man was talking, pausing, talking again, just like he was telling a story. She heard Con, too, but she almost didn't believe it was his voice.

Con was laughing!

Angie stepped cautiously into the room and saw Con propped up on two large pillows. There was a big grin on his face. She hadn't seen him smile like that since they were at La Mirada Beach together.

She hadn't been able to make him smile like that since the accident. Angie felt a sudden pang of jealousy. Whoever that man sitting in the chair was, she didn't like him. It wasn't fair that he should make Con act like his old self in one single visit, while she had been trying day after day.

"Come on in, Angie. Look who's here. Mr. Erickson, this is Angie. She's the one I told you about."

The man had his back to her. He got up slowly from his chair and turned so that Angie could see his face. She didn't recognize him, but she knew that Mr. Erickson was the athletic coach from Con's school. The one who had told Con he could get a scholarship—if he kept on running!

"Hello, Angie. I've heard a lot about you."

She held out her hand. "How do you do."

"Mr. Erickson's been telling me some funny stories about his experiences," Con said. "But, listen to this, Angie. He really thinks I'll be able to walk again. They have been trying to talk to me about it in therapy, but I . . . wouldn't listen."

Mr. Erickson smiled at Angie. "Artificial legs aren't what they used to be. They're much better. There's no reason why Con can't walk and finish his education . . . and have a career."

He went to the door; then he stopped and looked at Con. "Just remember what I told you, Con . . . about trusting. You have a lot of friends, but there's one who's with you twenty-four hours a day. The Lord isn't going to give you your own legs back, but he'll give you the strength to get along without them."

He lifted a hand and smiled at them both. Then he turned and walked down the hall. There was something unusual about the way he moved.

Angie noticed it, but not for long. She was too busy being mad at him. The idea of his coming in

here and building up Con's hopes. Artificial legs!
She knew what they were. Stumps of wood that
made hollow sounds on the sidewalk. She had seen
them on an old man who used to come to the mission. All the kids had laughed at him and called
him names. Angie shivered, remembering Stumpy
Sam.

Nobody knew what his real name was, and nobody ever asked. His pants were cut off at the
knees, and the wooden pieces stuck out like chair
legs where everybody could see them. When he
walked, he had to use crutches for balance. But you
couldn't really call it walking. He swung himself
along and rolled his body from side to side.

Oh, no! Con wasn't going to be like that. If he had
to stay in a wheelchair, at least he'd look . . . well,
dignified. And she was the one who would take
care of him. She would be his strength. They didn't
need Mr. Erickson—or anybody else.

"Hey, Angie! What're you looking so glum
about? Didn't you hear what the man said? I don't
have to stay in that contraption forever."

He pointed to the corner of the room near the
head of his bed where the collapsible wheelchair
was folded flat against the wall.

Angie didn't mind looking at it at all, and she
didn't mind seeing Con in it. When the nurse
tucked the blanket up around his waist, Angie
pretended that he was recovering from a long ill-
ness. The wheels were large and rolled so smoothly
that they could move down the hallway together
with only a soft whirring sound. She could push

145

him along and look down at the back of his sandy head and his broad shoulders and almost forget that so much of him was missing.

She didn't see why Con had never stopped hating it. He was looking at it right now as if he would like to throw it through the window.

"What's the matter with your wheelchair?" she asked. "Lots of people use wheelchairs."

"Not if they have another choice. Listen, Angie. I'm not trying to be funny or anything. But I really mean it when I say I'm not going to take this lying down. Or sitting, either. Not when there's a chance of standing up."

Standing up on wooden legs! Angie stuffed the flower in Flo's vase. Then she put both hands on her hips. "Mr. Erickson isn't a doctor, is he?"

"Of course not. But he knows a lot about artificial legs. He has one himself."

Mr. Erickson? Angie didn't believe it. Then she remembered the careful way he had gotten up from the chair and his slow, unhurried walk down the hall. But he didn't use crutches. He didn't even carry a cane.

"He doesn't walk like Stumpy Sam," she said out loud.

Con began to laugh. "Is that why you want to keep me in a wheelchair? So I won't walk like Stumpy Sam? Angie, I'm not talking about wooden legs. I'm talking about things called prostheses. Artificial limbs. It's a science, Angie. Dr. Stinson says it's really possible to make arms and legs. They're not skin and bone, and they're not as good

146

as the real things. But neither are false teeth—and millions of people get along with those just fine."

Angie didn't answer him. Con was looking at her with a puzzled expression on his face. "Hey!" he said. "What is this? You've been down in the mouth ever since you met Mr. Erickson."

For the first time in her life, Angie wished that she could talk about her feelings the way Con could. "I . . . thought he was getting your hopes up for nothing," she said. "You and I . . . we were doing OK, Con. I don't mind pushing you in a wheelchair. I thought . . . we didn't need him."

It wasn't the truth, and she knew it. Angie was down in the mouth because she was jealous. Jealous of Mr. Erickson, who had come here uninvited and made Con smile. She looked away from Con. He always had a way of figuring out what she was thinking.

It was too late. His face softened, and he reached for her hand. "You've been doing great, Angie. You're the one who has kept me going. But now it's time for me to get my act together. Something's happened to me, Angie. I can't explain it yet. But I feel good. I really feel like I'm going to make it."

He paused. "You do want me to walk again, don't you? You want us to be able to be together, the way we planned? Hey, Angie! Look at me! Do you feel different now . . . because I don't have any legs?"

How could she tell him what was inside of her? Of course she felt different. She wanted to take care of him now. She wanted to make it up to him. She *wanted* to push him in that chair. Most of all, she wanted to protect him from being hurt again.

How could she tell him he was in for a big disappointment? Maybe Mr. Erickson could walk pretty well, because he had only lost one leg. But Con didn't have any legs at all. Walking, for him, would be like using stilts. She was sure of it. She couldn't stand to think about the way he was going to look to other people.

Angie couldn't make herself tell him all these things. But he was waiting for an answer, and she could tell him what he wanted to hear.

"I feel the same way I always have . . . about you, Con." She could say that much. She loved Con. She always would.

He looked relieved. "Don't worry, Angie. I'm going to get out of here. I'm still going to get that scholarship. It won't be an athletic one, and I may have to work a little harder, but I'll get it. I'll pave the road for us, Angie, even if I have to do it on my hands and knees."

Then he started laughing.

"What's so funny?" she asked.

"I am. I can't seem to remember. I won't have to crawl, Angie. I'm going to walk!"

Angie laughed with him. She didn't want him to know that she had decided not to believe a word that Mr. Erickson had said.

14
THERAPY

During the next weeks Angie realized that Con was a different person. Oh, he still looked the same, but there was something about him. Even in his wheelchair, Angie thought he seemed bigger.

One day he came whirring down the hallway in his chair and found her sitting by his bed. This wasn't the first time he had been out of his room when she arrived.

"I'm sorry, Angie," he said. "I didn't mean to be so late, but . . ." Then he began to smile. "I've got a surprise for you, Angie."

She smiled back. It was good to see Con looking happy. "What is it?" she asked.

"Tomorrow you can come with me to therapy. It's OK for you to visit. You can see everything we do in there, Angie. You can finally see for yourself."

Then he reached out and gave her hand a squeeze. "Oh, Angie!" he said.

"Oh, Angie what?"

He laughed as if he had a secret. "I can't wait until tomorrow!"

But Angie could wait. She dreaded going to that place. The next afternoon she walked so slowly on her way to the hospital that she got there a lot later than usual. Con was sitting in his wheelchair in the hallway, looking impatient.

"I've been waiting for you," he said. "Come on. Let's get going." He gave the wheels a push that sent him rolling ahead of her down the hall. She hurried along behind him and tried not to feel irritated. Con had always let her push him in that chair. This was the first time he had scooted away from her like that.

She stepped into the elevator behind him and watched the doors slide shut. They moved slowly up, then up again. The doors opened, and Con wheeled himself out. A sign on the wall said Physical Therapy in large black letters, and an arrow pointed to the right.

Con scooted ahead of her again and led the way to the end of the hall where swinging double doors had been propped open to reveal a large room.

Angie came closer and looked in. This place wasn't what she had expected at all. It was like a gymnasium.

Con went through the doorway and motioned for her to follow. "I want you to meet someone," he said. "Angie, this is Joe Sullivan. He's a physical

150

therapist. He's also a pretty good friend."

Joe smiled. "Glad to meet you, Angie. Have you ever visited here before?"

Angie shook her head. "I wasn't sure I wanted to come. I didn't think it would look like this. I . . . I'm not sure what I thought."

Joe nodded. "That's the way it is with most people. Some of them are even afraid to come." He nodded toward Con. "We had a terrible time getting him in here. Now we can't get him out. Come on and have a look around."

They walked slowly through the room. Con seemed to know everybody, and it took a long time to stop and talk with each person. Some were lying on long tables, being massaged. Some were working with machines, pushing . . . pulling . . . strengthening muscles. A few were walking very slowly along short ramps with steel handgrips along the sides.

A row of mat exercisers filled one corner, and along the wall to Angie's right were parallel bars with mirrors. A young woman was moving carefully before them, watching herself critically as she walked.

Every one of the patients had a real problem. Sometimes Angie could tell what it was—like a missing arm or leg, and sometimes she could see that they were partially paralyzed. There were a few patients she just wondered about. But she knew they wouldn't be in here if there wasn't something wrong.

They made a complete circuit and came back to

the door. Con had stayed behind to talk to a friend, and Joe and Angie were standing together, waiting. "Well, what do you think?" Joe asked.

Angie hesitated. "I think . . . well, the thing that surprises me the most is how cheerful everybody is. How can they be so happy when they've lost so much?"

Joe looked thoughtful. "We try to tell people that they're still whole on the inside, and that's where it counts. That's what Con is learning, Angie. He's finding out he can be independent again. And he knows that sitting around saying 'Why me?' is a big waste of time."

"But he didn't deserve this," Angie said.

"That's not the point. Bad luck can happen to anybody. Life isn't a free ride, Angie, and it's no good feeling cheated when things don't go your way. You just have to pull yourself together and do the best you can with what you've got." He leaned over closer. "Con is finding out that he's a lot stronger than he thought he was. That's the first step to independence. And that's what Con needs most of all."

Angie thought about that all the way back to Con's room. She didn't try to push him this time, but watched him wheel himself along. He did it easily. Con didn't need pushing anymore.

Then what did Con need? And what was he doing about it? She had walked through the therapy room and seen all the equipment. But she hadn't seen Con using it. What did he do in there? What was happening to make him so happy?

152

She stood in front of his wheelchair. "Con, when you go to therapy, what do you do?"

It seemed to her that he was avoiding her eyes when he answered, "Oh, lots of things."

"Well, what things?"

"Lots of different exercises." He hesitated. "Especially arm exercises. You have to have strong arms to handle a wheelchair."

"So I noticed." She took a deep breath. "Con, have you given up trying to walk?"

He was really avoiding her now. "No . . . no, of course not. A thing like that takes a long time, that's all. Hey, look what time it is. Visiting hours are almost over."

Angie stared at him. He acted as if he wanted her to leave. But he wasn't mad at her. She could see the laughter in his eyes when he looked up and said, "See you tomorrow, Angie? Same time?"

She nodded. "If you're sure you want me to come."

This time the laughter bubbled right out of him. He grinned and took her hand. "Oh, I want you to come all right. You can't miss tomorrow."

Angie walked slowly to the elevator and pushed the button. She went downstairs and out into the still-warm air. She thought about Con all the way home, but she couldn't figure him out. The only thing she knew for sure was that he wasn't telling her everything. Con was acting like he had a secret.

15
ONE STEP AT A TIME

The next afternoon, Angie walked into Con's room and found his bed empty. There wasn't anything to do but sit in a chair and wait. She closed her eyes and listened. The hospital sounds were all familiar to her now. Especially the soft whirring of Con's wheelchair. She would be able to tell the minute he came through the door at the end of the hall.

But she didn't hear the sound of wheels at all. She heard the nurse's voice instead, right outside the door. "Wait a minute," Angie heard her say. "I'll see if she's here yet."

Angie opened her eyes and looked up at a white-capped head, poking around the edge of the door-way. "She's here all right," the nurse said. She gave Angie a wink and disappeared. In a second she was back. "Will you step out here into the hallway a minute?" she asked.

Angie got up and followed her out of the room. The nurse didn't say anything. She just pointed. Angie followed her finger.

Con was about halfway down the hall holding onto the railings of one of those three-sided steel frames with a seat across the back. But Con wasn't sitting. He was standing. And he was smiling at her.

Con standing! Angie closed her eyes, then looked again. She must be losing her mind. Con was wearing a blue T-shirt, and . . .

She looked quickly to where his legs should have been and saw the long pants. He was wearing Levis. There were brown shoes on his . . . No, that wasn't possible. For a second she felt a little dizzy and reached up her hand as if to cover her eyes.

Then Con did something she would never forget for the rest of her life. He took a careful step forward, then another, moving his left leg and then his right. He was walking. Con was standing up and walking. He was laughing at the same time.

"See!" He grinned at the nurses. "I told you she wouldn't be able to say a word."

The hallway was becoming crowded with people: nurses in white uniforms and doctors in green scrub suits. The doorways were filled with all the patients who were able to get out of bed to see Con walk. Angie knew they were there, and she knew they were clapping and cheering, but she really didn't see them. She didn't hear a thing except the sound of Con's voice saying over and over, "I'm coming, Angie."

She waited for him until he stood in front of her, just like Con had always stood—tall and strong. She looked up at his face and put the palm of her hand against his cheek and caught the single tear that fell.

She couldn't say anything for a long time; her throat was tight, and she was close to sobbing. She watched as the nurse helped him onto the bed and raised the back until he was sitting up against the pillows. Then she sat in a chair and wiped her eyes and looked at him.

"You walked," she finally said. "I saw you walk!"

"I've been doing it for quite a while, but I didn't want you to see me until I was sure I wouldn't fall on my face. I've been waiting to surprise you, Angie."

He reached down and gave the shapes beneath his pants a friendly pat. "These things are only temporary. They're like long posts with rubber feet . . . . How about that? Now I can stub my toe and it won't hurt! Do you want to see them?"

Angie smiled weakly. "Not right now; thanks just the same."

Con grinned. "I didn't want to see them, either. Not at first. But now they don't bother me at all." His voice quickened with excitement. "Just wait until I get the real things, Angie. Dr. Stinson says I can learn to walk quicker, because I still have one knee of my own."

He pointed to the walker. "I'll get rid of that thing as soon as I get my balance. Then I'll be on crutches for a while. Gee, that won't be any worse than two years ago when I broke my ankle. Remember?"

Angie remembered all right. He had complained the whole time. Now here he was, looking forward to doing the same thing. She looked at him lying there in the bed with his . . . prostheses that looked like legs under his Levis. Was it possible that Mr. Erickson had been telling the truth after all? Con would go back to school, and have a career. When she saw him the way he was now, it was hard *not* to believe it.

Angie felt like she needed to be quiet so she could think, but Con was pulling at her hand, demanding her attention. "Didn't you hear me, Angie? When I'm ready to throw away the crutches, they'll let me walk with a cane. Dr. Stinson says by the end of six months I can throw that away, too.

"And listen to this. I don't have to stay in the hospital all that time. I can go home in two more weeks, Angie. I can start school in September, just like I'd planned."

He stopped and took a long breath. He was squeezing her hand so hard it hurt. When he spoke again, his voice was low, but it had that urgent tone that she always recognized. It meant that he was about to tell her something important.

"Listen, Angie. I haven't told anybody else, but I want you to know what's been happening to me. After the accident, I used to lie here and pretend it wasn't true. But I couldn't keep that up very long, because I kept looking down and seeing that two big pieces of me were gone.

157

"So I tried something else. I kept remembering that neon sign over the mission that says PRAYER CHANGES THINGS, and I decided that I wanted it to change me. I prayed every night, Angie. I spent a lot of time telling God what I wanted him to do for me.

"Give me back my legs, Lord. I won't ever ask you for another thing, if you'll just give them back. But nothing happened. Not one darned thing.

"I felt worse and worse, until one night I couldn't sleep at all. Every time I closed my eyes, it seemed like I was sitting at the bottom of a deep well, with no rope to climb up on. I felt so low that I really didn't care what happened to me. There wasn't anything to do but give up.

"I said it right out loud: 'OK, God, my legs are gone, and I know I'm not going to grow any new ones. So let's try it your way. Just show me what it is you want me to do.'

"It seemed like somebody let down a rope and pulled me up where I could see daylight again. I opened my eyes, and it really was daylight. The sun was coming in through the window, and the darkness just drained out of me.

"I had given up, Angie, but I didn't feel like a quitter anymore. I felt like I was starting all over again . . . like I had decided to take another chance on life.

"Do you understand what I mean, Angie? Am I making any sense?"

Angie was beginning to feel pretty uncomfortable. Con was smiling at her, waiting for her to say something, and she didn't have any idea what to say. That was the trouble with Con. He thought a lot about things, and then he had to put his thoughts into words. He was good at that. But when he finished, he expected Angie to say something back. Usually she said all the wrong things, and it made him mad.

This time she decided to play it safe. "You always make sense," she told him, and she squeezed his hand hard. But, inside, she was confused. Suddenly she wanted to go home. She had a lot of things to think about. She squeezed Con's hand again. "I'll see you tomorrow," she said.

"One step at a time," he told her. "We're going to make it, Angie." He smiled tiredly. "I can go almost anywhere on these legs." Then he put his head on the pillow and closed his eyes.

Angie closed hers, too. She remembered when he had said those same words on a rooftop, about a million years ago.

She waited until she was sure he was sleeping, then tiptoed out of the room. She went quickly down the hall to the elevator and pushed the button. She was outside on the hospital steps when she remembered something Con had said. It jumped forward out of her mind and dangled like a puppet on a string. He was coming home in two weeks. Home to Bundy Street.

That's what Dr. Stinson had told him. But Dr. Stinson didn't know that Con's home was a deserted apartment on the second floor. He didn't know about Orly. Or about Con's mother who didn't care. Angie thought of the other room at the top of the stairs, with the sleeping bag on the floor and the magazine that said, "Keep Running!" She knew Con couldn't stay there.

She also knew what happened to minors who were deserted by their parents. They got put into foster homes. Angie began walking faster. Suddenly she began to run. She had to find a place for Con to live. They would take him away. She'd never see him again. Con didn't even know it, she thought, but he still needed her. *He does need me. I know he does.*

She was aware of people on the street. She went around them and between them, and then she saw the workman who was just ahead, repairing a ten-foot strip of sidewalk. He saw her coming just in time and stepped aside.

Angie saw the wet cement, but it was too late. She stepped in it . . . skidded . . . felt it ooze over the tops of her sneakers. Angie took a large step sideways onto dry concrete and looked back over her shoulder.

"You kids never look where you're going, do ya? You don't care two hoots about anybody but yourselves!" The workman's voice was loud and angry.

"That's not true. Look, mister, I'm sorry. I really am. I just didn't see you. I was thinking . . ."

"Get out of here. Go on. Git!" He raised a shovel in the air and took a step forward.

Angie backed away, then turned and tried to run. She couldn't. Her feet were covered with wet cement. She went around a corner and leaned against a low wall. She couldn't sit on it, because there were iron spokes sticking out of the top.

That's the way things always were, she thought. Something was always poking up and getting in your way. Well, she was sick of it. Joe Sullivan had been right about one thing. Life wasn't a free ride, and it wasn't a smooth one, either. It didn't do you any good to try to hurry. All you got for your efforts was wet cement all over your feet.

Angie was breathing slower now. She reached down to the sidewalk and picked up a pointed stick and began to dig the cement from her shoes. She kept thinking about what Con had said. In her own mind she had always connected God with that statue of George Washington on top of the mission. She had always thought that believing in him was a little like believing in the president. You knew he existed, but you never had a chance to get acquainted.

Con had made it all sound different. He acted almost like he had really been introduced and had a chance to shake hands. Angie poked at her shoe angrily. God might be on Con's side. She wasn't going to argue about that. But she was the one who was going to have to find a place for Con to live.

She threw away the stick and started walking down the street. She was beginning to limp a little on one foot, where the cement had hardened on the inside of her shoe. She was probably getting a blister, but it wasn't going to slow her down.

The dried cement made crunching sounds on the bottoms of her shoes, but Angie pulled her shoulders back and walked a little faster. She wasn't going to be a quitter, either. You had to be a fighter to survive in this world, and that's what she intended to be.

She just wished she could bury the thought at the edge of her mind that kept telling her that she was sinking into a deep well.

16
THE LOCKED DOOR

When Angie came up the front steps of the apartment building, she saw that the front door was ajar. Voices were coming from just inside. She didn't mean to eavesdrop, but she couldn't seem to help it. Tony and her mother were talking together.

"I've got to get the girls out of here, Tony."

"I know how you feel, Evelyn. But how do you think you're going to manage that? Moving takes money."

Angie stopped on the top step. Her mother couldn't mean that. They couldn't leave Bundy Street now. Not when Con needed a home. Then she heard Tony's voice again. She had never heard him sound that way before.

"Evelyn . . ."

Just one word. That was all he said. It hung on the air like a question mark until her mother wiped it away with a single sentence.

"Tony, I . . . have an aunt back East. I've told you about her."

Angie knew who that would be. Her name was Aunt Martha, and she lived in Massachusetts. Every Christmas she sent them a box that contained ugly, black, hand-knit stockings. Angie's mother always said it was the thought that counted, and that Aunt Martha was a good woman, but Angie wondered about that.

Tony laughed, but it wasn't a happy sound. "Ha!" he said. "You've told me about her all right. Isn't she the one who wouldn't let you come home after Frank died?"

Angie stood absolutely still. Now she was listening on purpose. Frank was her father's name. But he hadn't died. Tony had the story all wrong.

"Aunt Martha never approved of Frank," her mother answered. "The hard part is that she was right. When things got tough for him, he just walked out on us. She knew he would never come back, and I knew it, too. Just the same, it was a shock when I heard he was killed in an accident. Tony, I . . . never told the girls. I suppose I'll have to someday. But it will be like telling them a stranger died, because they never really knew him."

For a few seconds, Angie didn't hear another thing. Her ears were ringing, and she had to concentrate hard to catch her mother's next words.

"She offered to take the girls. I never told you that part, Tony. Aunt Martha said she never wanted to see me again, because I had disobeyed her, but she would be willing to see that the girls got a proper upbringing."

Angie felt a cold chill go right down her back. She would never live with Aunt Martha. Never! But the worst thing was that her mother had lied to her . . . and to Caro, too. The old dream flashed through her head and disappeared like a burned-out light bulb—all in one big flash. She leaned against the porch railing and listened to their voices.

"I wrote to Aunt Martha today, Tony. I asked her to let them come and stay. They don't have a chance here on Bundy Street."

"Evelyn . . ." Tony sounded like he had a sore throat. "Families should be together."

"We will be together as soon as I get a better job. I need to go back to school, Tony. I can rent a single room, and work nights and study days. I used to type pretty well. All I need is a little shorthand. Later, I'll get a better place to live, and I'll send for the girls, and we'll all be . . ."

"Wait a minute. . . . You're not thinking straight, because you're upset. You said you were miserable growing up in your aunt's house. How do you think your girls will feel?"

Her voice was stiff when she answered. It was the same voice she used on Angie when she didn't want to talk about something anymore. "I know what's best for them, and it's not living here. Anyway, it's too late. I've already written the letter."

Tony's voice was so low Angie could hardly hear him. "Have you thought what this will do to Con?"

There was a long silence. "I can't help it," her mother finally said. "I just can't see any other way."

Angie bit the inside of her cheek. How she hated being thirteen. If she were only a few years older, she could . . . She was so angry she didn't realize that the talking had stopped. Suddenly, her mother and Tony were standing on the porch, looking at her.

"How long have you been listening, young lady?" her mother demanded.

She hated it when her mother called her that. "Long enough," she said defiantly.

"Listen, Angie." Her mother's voice softened. "We need to talk. I want you to understand . . ."

Angie shook her head. "If you want to get rid of Caro and me, I guess there isn't anything we can do about it, is there? But maybe you can tell me where Con is going to live when we're gone." Her voice rose. "They're letting him out of the hospital in two weeks. You didn't know that, did you? When they find out he doesn't even have an address, they'll put him in a foster home, and you won't even care!"

She was yelling. She was being rude and horrible, and she was glad. She took a deep breath and got ready for a whole lot more. But Tony stepped in and ruined the whole thing.

"Con does have an address, Angie. He's coming to my place."

Angie let her breath out in one whoosh. "He can't do that," she protested.

"Why not?"

"Because . . . they'll find out you're not his father. Then they'll come and take him away."

"They already know the whole story," Tony told her. "Listen, Angie, you don't have to worry about a foster home, because Tony's Deli is the foster home they're sending Con to. He wanted it to be a surprise."

Angie looked from one of them to the other. She knew she ought to feel glad, but she didn't. They'd done this behind her back. It wasn't a surprise. It was just plain sneaky. She hated them for it.

"I've had enough surprises for one day," she said. Then she stepped around Tony and walked past her mother without another word.

"Just one minute . . ." her mother began.

"Leave her alone, Evelyn," Tony said. His voice was tired, and he sounded discouraged. "You go on to work so you won't be late."

Angie kicked the door shut behind her so she couldn't hear their voices anymore. The apartment was empty. That meant Caro was still at Flo's. Good. She didn't want to talk to anybody right now.

She went into the kitchen and stared at the refrigerator, remembering what her mother had said to her before she left for the hospital. "If you don't pick up some powdered milk on your way home, there won't be any for dinner tonight."

Well, she hadn't, and there wasn't. So what?

Angie reached into the cupboard and took out a jar of instant coffee. She would make a cup, and she would drink it black. Nobody was going to stop her. She couldn't think of anybody who cared.

She opened the jar and measured out two heaping spoonfuls. Then she boiled water and poured it into the cup. The coffee was strong and bitter and so hot it burned her tongue. She drank some anyway; then she pushed the cup aside.

She sat at the table and stared straight ahead. She felt as if she were wearing somebody else's glasses. There were colors and shapes in front of her, but she didn't see them clearly. Gradually, one of the colors grew brighter and took shape. She forced her eyes to focus on it.

It was the red plastic geranium in the kitchen window. It was a fake, she thought, hating it. "Fake!" she said out loud. "Fake, like Con's legs. Fake, like everything else around this place."

She pounded her fist hard on the table. The coffee sloshed out of the cup and made a dark pool on the shiny Formica surface. Angie didn't bother to clean it up. She got up and dumped the contents of her cup into the sink. A dark, oily scum formed over the cold, white enamel. When she flushed it with water, it didn't wash away.

Angie looked at it and began to cry. She didn't make a sound, but the tears ran down her face and into her mouth. She reached up for the red geranium with both hands and pulled it from the pot. Tiny clods of dirt exploded into the sink and mixed with the wet coffee scum.

Angie stared at them. Boy, was that funny! Her mother had planted that fake geranium in real dirt. She walked to the wastebasket and dropped it in. Then she reached in with her hands and buried it beneath the other trash. She never wanted to see it again.

Angie went into the bathroom and washed her hands and face. When Caro came back from Flo's, Angie took enough meat out of the refrigerator to make two hamburger patties. There weren't any buns, so she put them between pieces of white bread, spread with mustard and catsup. You had to hold them over your plate, so they wouldn't drip down your arms.

Then she watched television with Caro and listened to her talk about everything she had done that day. Caro told it all at least four times. They pulled the bed out so Caro could lie down while she watched television. She wasn't tired, she told Angie. But before it was dark outside, she had closed her eyes.

Angie turned the television down to a murmur, watched Caro for a minute to make sure she wasn't pretending, and then slipped quietly out the door.

She knew exactly where she was going. She climbed the stairs quickly, almost at a run, because she didn't want to talk to anybody on the way. She needn't have worried. People on Bundy Street didn't spend their summer evenings on inside stairways. They went out into the street where they could breathe.

Angie could breathe best up on the roof. It was

quiet up there. She needed to be quiet. She had a lot to think about.

But she didn't think. She leaned against the low wall and watched as the city lights blinked on one at a time. She felt the salty breeze as it blew cool air inland from the ocean. And later, when the sky turned darker, she counted stars in a cloudless sky.

She tried to empty her mind of everything, especially the things that had happened that afternoon. She tried to tip her brain over and let everything run out, just like she had dumped the bitter black coffee from her cup into the sink. But no matter how hard she tried, there was always some scum left in the bottom. She didn't know what to use to wash it out. Even worse, she didn't know what she would fill it with if it was clean.

She sat down on the floor of the roof and leaned her back against the wall. Little questions wiggled in the corners of her mind, like tiny worms eating through the core of an apple.

Why did she resent Con's independence? Why had she been so hateful to Tony? Why couldn't she try to understand what her mother had done?

Angie had never wished for a father as hard as she wished for one right now. Everything would be different if she had a father to talk to. She could go to him when she was in trouble. She wouldn't feel like she had to figure out everything all by herself.

Angie closed her eyes and willed the old dream back one more time. She made her father walk down the street and up the front steps. She made him tap three times on the door. In her mind,

Angie stood there with her hands sweating and her heart beating hard. Then she reached out and turned the knob as she always did.

But this time nothing happened. The door was locked. Angie twisted the knob and pulled hard, but it wouldn't open. He was there, but he couldn't get in. She heard him knocking on the other side of the door. She didn't want him to be a stranger.

"Father . . ." she called. Then louder, "Father . . ."

She opened her eyes quickly and looked around. She was alone on the rooftop. The voice she had heard was her own. She had said the words out loud, and no one had answered her. But for a few short seconds, Angie had felt like someone really was there. Someone who could help her figure things out or throw her a rope if she fell into a deep well.

That's what Con had said. But Con hadn't been talking about her father. He had been talking about God.

Could God be a father? There was a prayer that started out like that. *Our Father, who art in heaven* . . . Angie had never really thought of God like that. He'd always seemed more like the George Washington statue over the mission. Big, and a little frightening.

A real father wouldn't be that way. He would be someone who was there when you needed him. He would be warm and loving. He would never give up, even when you did.

What was it that Con had said? You can give up

without being a quitter. Angie didn't see how. But the way she felt tonight, giving up seemed like the only thing left for her to do.

She leaned her head back against the face of the wall and closed her eyes. She sat very still. "OK," she said out loud. "I give up."

She kept her eyes closed and waited. She waited for about fifteen minutes. Con had said it was like a miracle for him. But Angie didn't feel a thing.

Finally, she said it louder, just in case God hadn't heard her. "I . . . GIVE . . . UP!"

But nothing happened. Nothing at all.

Angie stood up and stamped her foot. "What is it you want me to do? What do you expect, anyway? Do you want me to get down on my knees and tell you how helpless I am? Well, I am not helpless. So how do you like that?"

Nobody answered. Angie hadn't really expected a booming voice out of the sky. But she had hoped for some kind of a sign. Maybe she had made God mad. That might be the reason nothing happened.

But Angie knew that wasn't true. The real reason was that stupid locked door inside her head. No matter how hard she pulled on it, she didn't know how to make it open. In her mind she saw it, growing taller and wider, and it was so thick she didn't see how anyone could break it down.

She looked up at the stars. It seemed more likely to her that God would be there than down on Bundy Street. "Show me how to open the door," she whispered. "Please show me how."

The night winds blew across the rooftop. But

they didn't tell her a thing. A cat howled somewhere in one of the yards below, and the 10:05 bus screeched its brakes at Chico's corner. Briefly, like a candle flickers when it's about to go out, she saw a light in the old abandoned house at the end of the street.

Angie shivered. She must have imagined that. Nobody ever went in that place. She walked slowly across the roof, climbed down to the narrow balcony at the back of the house, and went through the door into the room at the top. There weren't any answers for her tonight. Even if there were, she thought she was so tired she probably wouldn't have understood them.

She went down the stairs to the front door, opened it, and stepped out onto the front porch. The long, tangled weed that had been growing there for several weeks had twined, like ivy, all the way up one of the mortuary columns. Angie looked at it closely; then she reached out to touch a long, milky-white bud. It broke off and lay in her palm.

The bud felt soft and strange against her skin, like cool silk. She began to pull it apart, starting with the tissuey folds at the tip. It tore, revealing a deep, bright purple center: a five-pointed star connected by delicate lavender webbing.

Angie stared at it a second; then she reached out and dropped it over the edge of the porch. There was a stickiness still on her palm when she opened the front door and went back inside. It was the only door she was able to open. It was her own address.

On Bundy Street.

17
GUIDELINES

In the morning, when Angie opened the front door of the apartment building, Jessica was sitting on the front steps. Angie almost went back in and closed the door. She hadn't seen Jessica since that day at the skating rink. The day when Jessica had called Bundy Street a slum, and all Angie's troubles had started.

Jessica was sitting like she always did with her chin on her hands and her elbows on her knees. And she was looking up and down Bundy Street with an expression of superiority.

At least that's what Angie supposed she was doing. She couldn't really see anything but the back of her head. Jessica's straw-colored hair looked as if it had just been ironed. It hung straight down her back and was cut even around the edges. She parted it in the middle and pushed it behind her ears, which wasn't such a great idea, because Jessica's ears were really big. Angie clicked the door shut and watched Jessica turn around.

"What're you doing here?" Angie asked. "Is this your day for slumming?"

"Cut it out, Angie. Why do you always have to carry a grudge?"

"Look, Jessica, you're the one who started the whole thing."

"OK. OK. I'm sorry. I'm apologizing. Are you happy now?"

Angie shrugged and went to sit on the top step. A few weeks ago she would have felt like taking a handful of Jessica's yellow hair and pulling it hard. But she didn't feel like it this morning.

"I heard about Con."

Angie nodded. "I guess everybody has."

"I . . . thought I might go see him in the hospital."

Angie didn't answer.

Jessica cleared her throat. "I was just wondering if . . . he'd want to see me or not."

Angie glanced at her. Jessica kept pulling her hair back behind her ears. She did it over and over, as if it wouldn't stay there. Angie wished she would quit it. It was making her nervous.

"Listen, Angie . . ." Jessica looked at her and put her hands in her lap. But she couldn't seem to hold them still. Slowly and methodically, she began cracking her knuckles. "You don't think Con ran away with Took because of what I said . . . do you, Angie?"

Angie was startled. "Because of what you said?" Nothing Jessica said would ever matter to Con. He didn't pay any attention to her.

"You know—about Bundy Street being a slum." Jessica turned her head away just enough so that Angie couldn't see her face. She was pretending to look at something interesting down the street, but there wasn't anything there to see except Corky's Parking Lot, and there wasn't anything unusual about that.

Angie leaned forward a little. "What are you staring at?"

"Nothing!" Jessica's voice was sharp. "I'm just asking you a simple question."

Then Angie saw Jessica bite her lip. She couldn't believe it. Jessica Smith, who thought she was better than anybody, was about to lose her cool.

"I can't stand it anymore, Angie," she said. "Ever since I heard about the accident, I've been thinking about that day. I keep wondering if . . . any of it was my fault."

She stopped and wiped her face on her shirt sleeve. "If it was my fault that he left, then . . . don't you see . . . it could be my fault that he doesn't have any legs."

Her voice squeaked like a mouse in a trap, and she buried her face in her lap. Angie had never liked Jessica very much, and she couldn't honestly say that she liked her any better now, while she was snuffling. But she had to admit that she felt sorry for her. Angie knew exactly how she felt. She waited a minute; then she reached out a hand and reluctantly put it on Jessica's shoulder.

"Hey, Jessica," she said. "You don't need to feel that way. Con didn't pay any attention to what you said. Come on, Jess. It really wasn't your fault. It wasn't anybody's fault."

Except Took's. Mentally, Angie subtracted his name from her list of anybodies. As far as she was concerned, he didn't classify.

Jessica looked up. Her nose was red, her eyes were puffy, and her hair hung like twisted spaghetti around her face. "You're just telling me that to make me feel better," she said.

"For pete's sake, Jess. Why would I do a thing like that? I don't even like you."

Jessica brightened. "That's right, you don't. So I guess I can believe you." She looked at Angie a minute. "I don't like you, either. But I don't not like you as much as I used to."

Angie nodded. "I know what you mean." She suddenly felt generous. "I think Con might like it if you came by the hospital," she told her.

Jessica pulled her hair back behind her ears again and stood up. She pulled a handkerchief out of her pocket and wiped her eyes. She always carried a handkerchief. It was one of the things that made her different. Then she pointed at the climbing vine. "Who planted that?" she asked.

Angie stared at it. It looked as if it had grown several inches since yesterday, and it was full of buds, like the one she had picked last night. "Nobody planted it. It's just some kind of weed," she said.

Jessica shook her head firmly. "That's no weed. It looks like a morning-glory vine. The flowers last one day, but they only open up when the sun shines. Gee, Angie, they make lots of seeds. You could have morning glories all over Bundy Street by next year."

Jessica really was a little crazy. Angie was remembering the fake geranium that she had buried in the trash last night. There was one just like it in a cracked pot on the front porch. That was the only kind of flower that grew here. She suddenly had a vision of fake red geraniums growing on vines all over Bundy Street. Fake geraniums planted in real dirt. She started to laugh.

"That would be something to look at," she said. "Bundy Street, covered with flowers. People would come from miles around."

"I don't see what's so funny about it. It could really happen."

"Jessica, I've never seen a real flower on this street . . . except for the ones in Old Lu's cart."

Jessica shrugged and started down the steps. "That's probably because nobody planted any." She walked a few steps; then she turned and came back. "I almost forgot to tell you. Took's mother is looking for him."

"Took's mother! I never knew he had a mother!"

"Don't be silly, Angie."

"Well, she must not worry about him too much. He's been missing since the night of the accident."

Jessica shrugged. "You know how it is. Took isn't the kind of person to check in every night. But after a couple of weeks his mother began to think it was kind of strange. She says he always used to come home when he got hungry. She'll give him a few more days, and then she's going to report him to the police."

Angie looked at Jessica carefully. She seemed to know an awful lot about Took. If she was telling the truth, he was about to become a missing person after all.

"I've gotta go," Jessica said. She stood on the sidewalk looking at Angie. "See you around?" she asked.

Angie hesitated. A few weeks ago, she would have answered automatically: "Get lost, Jessica." It would have been as simple as that. But things were different between them now. They weren't friends. But things were definitely different. Angie raised both shoulders and let them drop. "Sure," she answered. "Why not?"

Then she watched Jessica walk down Bundy Street towards Chico's corner. She watched her twitch her yellow hair from side to side and point her nose in the air just the way she always did. Angie used to hate the way Jessica walked, but it didn't seem to bother her today. Maybe it was the only way Jessica knew how to walk.

The door slammed behind her, and Caro came out on the porch and gave her a nudge. "You ready to go to Flo's?" she asked.

"It's too early. Anyway, I have to talk to Tony. Why don't you go on ahead?"

Angie knew why Caro was in a hurry. Flo had

put her in charge of all the potted plants at Maria's. She must have a green thumb, Flo had explained, because the plants were growing. Pretty soon they would be filling the windows and touching the floor, and the customers from uptown would think they were eating in a greenhouse.

Caro wasn't satisfied with just gardening at Flo's. A few days ago Angie had seen her walking up and down the street with water-filled milk cartons, pouring a little liquid on each dusty, wire-protected tree.

Angie leaned over, curiously, and looked at the base of the morning-glory vine. Just as she had thought Caro had watered that, too. The crack in the concrete was a fairly large one, and she must have poured a lot of water into it, because it was still damp around the surface. No wonder the silly vine was growing. Caro was turning into the Florence Nightingale of Bundy Street, only she was carrying water instead of a lantern.

A chattering noise across the street made her look toward the Deli. Tony had pulled a ladder onto the sidewalk, and he was beginning to wash the display window at the front of his store. Bandit's rope was looped around the leg of the ladder. The little monkey perched on the warm sidewalk and rubbed his tiny hands in the soapy water.

Angie got up and started slowly across the street. She had to talk to Tony, but she wasn't exactly sure what she was going to say.

"Hi!" It seemed a safe enough way to start.

"Morning, Angie." Tony kept right on washing.

Angie reached over and scratched Bandit behind his little ears. He gave a shriek and jumped to the ledge. Then he looked at Tony and began copying him, rubbing the glass with his wet paws.

"That window doesn't look dirty to me," Angie said. "What are you washing it for?"

Tony looked over his shoulder. "Do you wait until you're good and dirty before you take a bath?" He rubbed hard on a smudge. "Clean windows make me feel good. Maybe someday the rest of Bundy Street will take the hint."

Angie leaned against the doorway and watched him. "It'll take more than clean windows to change things around here," she said.

He climbed down from the stepladder. To her surprise he held up his index finger and shook it in her face. "Clean windows are a good start," he said. "And washing them is better than complaining about them."

He turned around and swung the ladder up under one arm and picked up the bucket of water in the other hand. For a second, Bandit was free. The little monkey didn't waste any time, but headed next door, straight for the sunbather, who spent most of every warm day with his legs stretched across the sidewalk in front of the mission. Bandit landed, with a plop, right on his lap and began to wash the man's face with his soapy paws.

"Help!" the man yelled. "Somebody get this monster off me!"

Angie had never seen the man look alive before. He was always in the same spot on sunny days, but she had never seen him come, and she had never seen him go.

But he looked alive now. He jumped straight up in the air. His eyes and mouth were open, and he was waving his arms around over his head. Bandit hung tightly to the man's jacket. His tail swung wildly, reaching for something to hold on to, and his little voice shrieked in fear.

Tony dropped everything and ran to the rescue. "Cut that out!" he yelled. "You're scaring my monkey!"

Bandit gave a jump and landed in Tony's arms. He grabbed Tony around the neck and held on tight. The bucket of soapy water had spilled, and a pool began to form in front of the mission. The sunbather pointed at the wet sidewalk and began to shout.

"Now look what you've done! How do you expect me to sit out here?"

Tony calmly lifted up his index finger. He was getting pretty handy with it, Angie thought, as he thrust it right in the sunbather's face. "I don't expect you to sit at all. Now that you've shown us how fast you can move, why don't you stay on your feet and do something useful? You've had a lot of free soup in that mission, haven't you?"

The sunbather looked uncomfortable. He began to shuffle his feet. ". . . not my fault . . . no money . . ."

"You've got *time*, haven't you?" Tony pointed to the cracked stucco and the gold paint peeling from the statue. "Just look at that! I happen to know

that a little paint and plaster would fix all of it . . .
if anybody cared enough to try."

The sunbather looked down at his shoes. "Where
would I get paint and plaster?"

"Inside!" Tony's voice came out like thunder.
"Inside the mission. In the storeroom off the
kitchen. I donated it myself when George Washington first began to peel!"

The man stepped back, looked up at the statue,
and stared. "Is that George Washington?" he
asked. He sounded amazed, and Angie thought it
was probably the first time he had looked up
higher than the sidewalk.

Angie and Tony left him standing there. They
went into the Deli, Tony going first, with the ladder and Bandit, and Angie following, carrying the
empty bucket.

She didn't say anything for a while. Just sat on a
stool and watched as Tony got ready to open up the
store. He was acting different this morning, bang-
ing things around and slamming cupboards, like
he was mad at somebody. She wished he would
look at her, but he just went about his business.
Angie slipped from her stool and went to the little
round table that Tony kept for customers who
wanted to sit down and eat a sandwich.

The table was in a corner that was decorated
with posters of Italy on the walls. Between two
bright posters was a black frame. Behind the glass
were some words written in heavy black ink.
Angie leaned forward to read them.

I went to the woods because I wished to live

deliberately . . . and not, when I came to die, discover that I had not lived.

Beneath the words was the author's name. Thoreau. She knew about Thoreau. They had studied him in school. She read the words again. Was that the way Tony felt? Did he want to go and live in the woods like Thoreau had?

She turned around to ask him and found that he was already standing right behind her. He put his arm around her shoulders and she saw, with relief, that he was the old Tony—the one she could talk to—not an angry stranger who muttered and slammed drawers.

She wanted to say she was sorry about the awful way she had acted last night. She wanted to tell him she was glad that Con was coming here to live. But she didn't. She opened her mouth, and something else came out.

"Oh, Tony, why did my mother lie to me? Why did she tell me my father had to go away? I've been waiting all this time, Tony. I thought he would be coming back."

"Listen, Angie, your mother didn't want you to be hurt."

Angie gave a little laugh. "She doesn't want me at all. Or Caro, either. We're in her way. That's why she wants us to go to live with Aunt Martha."

"You know that's not true. Your mother loves you both. She's just worried, because of what happened to Con—and because she thinks your Aunt Martha can give you a good home and things your mother can never afford."

184

"Like long black stockings? . . . Well, I'm not going, Tony. If my mother doesn't want us, we won't stay in her way. But we're not going to Massachusetts, either. Caro and I are . . . running away."

It wasn't true, and she knew it. But she felt better because she had said it.

Tony sighed and sat down hard on one of the little white metal chairs; then he motioned her into the other one. "There isn't any such thing as running away, Angie. Wherever we go, we take our problems with us. And we only find someplace else we have to run away from." He pointed to the words on the wall. "That's what Thoreau was talking about. We all have to stop somewhere and take a stand on what we believe in. We have to live on purpose, Angie. Deliberately."

"But . . . things happen, Tony. Things you don't plan on. How can you live on purpose when your life is all messed up?"

"You just look around you and face facts, and then you see what you can do to change things to make them better."

"You mean like praying about them? Don't give me that, Tony. Prayer doesn't change a thing. I tried it, and it doesn't work for me."

He leaned back in his chair until it balanced on two legs. "I'll bet it doesn't . . . if you only pray for things."

She looked at him suspiciously. "What are you getting at?"

"Prayer changes people, Angie. And people can

work together to change things. That's what living on purpose is all about."

He reached out and took hold of her hands. "Look, honey, things don't always turn out the way we plan them. Man's free will is a great gift, but sometimes it gets us into trouble. That's why we need a lot of guidance. It's there, if we just ask for it. It helps us make responsible decisions. . . Angie, it keeps us from running away."

Angie shrugged. "So, what am I supposed to do now? Make the best of Massachusetts?"

He looked at her a long time. "You're not in Massachusetts yet. You might try making the best of Bundy Street. Now wait a minute, Angie! Don't make a long face like that. Bundy Street does have possibilities. Just because part of a city grows old, that doesn't mean it has to become a slum. There are lots of good things about Bundy Street. Just look how people have shown they care about Con."

"But how can you change the rest of it? The dirty sidewalks, and the cracks in the walls, and the . . ."

Tony held up his hand for silence. "Listen!"

There was a strange, scraping sound coming from somewhere outside, on the front side of the building. Tony went quickly to the doorway and looked out. Then he took a few steps across the sidewalk and looked up toward the top of the mission.

"Come here, Angie," he called.

Angie stood beside him and stared up at the gold statue on top of the neon sign. The sunbather had propped a tall ladder against the front of the building and was standing on it, while he chipped flaking gold paint away from George Washington's coat. On the ledge beside him sat two cans of paint and a large, thick brush.

"Angie, my girl, you start with something small . . . like washing a window. Then you give a few gentle hints . . ."

Angie had to smile. She didn't think Tony's hints to the sunbather had been so gentle. Then she found the courage to ask him a question.

"What were you so mad about this morning, Tony?"

His mustache twitched when he answered. "I was mad at your mother, Angie, for wanting to leave. And I was mad at myself for not having the courage to tell her how I feel . . . about all of you."

Angie stared at him. How did he feel? She waited for him to tell her, but his mustache twitched again, and he turned without another word and went inside to wait on a customer.

18
CHAIN REACTION

Angie thought a lot about what Tony had said. She worked at Flo's and visited Con and came back to Bundy Street and sat on the top step and thought some more. But she didn't ask Tony, and she didn't say a thing about it to her mother when she left for work. She didn't want to ruin the hope by putting it into words before she was sure it was true. Tony and her mother? Just thinking about it made her happy and scared at the same time. What if Tony never mentioned it again? What if they all moved away, and Tony never said anything at all?

By the next morning she had decided what she was going to do. She was going to tell Caro about Aunt Martha. Then the two of them were going to start a chain reaction, even if they had to do all the reacting themselves. She wasn't exactly sure how they were going to start, but she knew one thing.

They had to show their mother that Bundy Street wasn't a slum. They had to make her want to stay here, with them . . . with Tony . . . and with Con.

Angie waited until she and Caro were alone that night. "I have something important to tell you," she said. "It's about Aunt Martha."

Caro made a sour face. Then she began to look worried. "She's not coming out here, is she?"

"No. It's worse than that. We may have to go and live with her. Mom already wrote a letter, asking if it's all right."

Caro squinted her eyes and looked at Angie through the slits. "You're making that up."

"No, I'm not. She really wrote it. I heard her tell Tony. She's afraid if we stay here, something bad will happen to us, like it did to Con. She wants us to get out of this neighborhood right now."

Caro turned white. "It's a dump all right. I used to want to leave, but now . . ."

Angie knew she was thinking about how much she loved mom, and about working at Flo's, and Con coming home, and Tony, and Bandit.

"I know." She nodded. "The place has its good points after all. Even if it didn't, I wouldn't want to go and live with Aunt Martha and wear those long black stockings, would you?"

Caro looked scared. She shook her head.

"Then there's only one thing for us to do," Angie told her.

"You mean, run away?"

"No, silly! I said that to Tony, but I didn't mean it. It's a dumb idea. You have to figure out what to do about your problems right where you find them, and our problem is Bundy Street. Listen, Caro, Jessica came by here this morning, and she said . . ."

"Jessica?"

"That's right. Let me finish. She said that weed on the front porch is really a flower that makes lots of seeds. She said they could spread, and we might have flowers all over Bundy Street.

"Well, I laughed at her and told her I'd never seen any real flowers here, except the ones for sale on Old Lu's cart. You know what she told me? She said that's just because nobody ever planted any."

Caro pursed her lips. "I thought you said Jessica was stupid."

Angie sighed. "She is stupid. But she's not quite as stupid as I thought. She was right about one thing. Bundy Street is the way it is, because nobody ever planted any seeds before."

She saw the light in Caro's eyes and knew she understood. "You mean idea seeds," Caro exclaimed. "Like cleaning things up, and . . . watering the trees . . . and washing the Deli window. Angie! Tony and I planted seeds yesterday!"

Angie nodded. "Some of them are already starting to sprout. George Washington is getting a new coat of gold paint."

"Oh, Angie. Do you think we can clean the whole street up before Con comes home? We only have two weeks."

Two weeks. It would take a miracle to change Bundy Street in two weeks. But Angie didn't say so. She just smiled at Caro and turned out the light.

In the morning, Angie took her mother's broom; then she went next door and borrowed Flo's for Caro to use. They started on opposite sides of the street: Caro in front of Pete's Parking and Angie in front of the deserted house on the corner. There was something about that place that bothered Angie, especially since she had seen a light flickering in one of the windows. No one would want to live in a place like that. But she had seen the light. She was sure she hadn't imagined it.

She started to sweep fast, because she was thinking about the rats that Flo said lived there and she didn't want to meet one of them. When she came to Flo's, the door opened, and Flo's curler-adorned head stuck out.

"What are you kids up to?" she demanded.

"We're sweeping. It's supposed to give people ideas. You know, get them interested in cleaning up Bundy Street."

Flo looked puzzled. "For pity's sake!" she exclaimed. She closed the door, but Angie could see her through the front window of Maria's, standing in the middle of the room. She had her index finger in the center of her chin, the way she always did when she was thinking.

Angie swept past the apartments, moving a little slower now. By the time she had finished the front of Hoang Chou's and explained what she was doing, her arms ached, and she felt like sitting down. When she reached Chico's, the palms of her hands were burning, and the dust from the sidewalk was making her sneeze.

Across the street, Tony was helping Caro sweep up the mess of gold paint chips that covered the sidewalk in front of the mission. George Washington gleamed brightly above them, but the sunbather was nowhere to be seen. While Angie watched, he appeared, coming from inside the mission, carrying a sack of concrete mix.

"Hey! What's goin' on out here?" Chico stood behind her in the little alley. He was just arriving for the day, and had parked his car in back.

Angie took her broom and swept it hard over the top of the picnic table. Black flies rose in the air and buzzed angrily. Then they settled back again like a solid black cloud. Chico's face looked a little like a black cloud, too. For a second Angie was scared, but only for a second. This was just Chico. She'd known him all her life.

"I'm sweeping," she said meekly.

"I can see that," he muttered. "Why don't you go and sweep on your own property?"

"I already did that." Angie bit her lip. Chico was no dummy. And he was proud. She decided to tell him the truth: all about Aunt Martha and trying to make things look better before Con came home.

He listened to her, and gradually he stopped frowning. But he still had a serious look on his face when he said, "Maybe your mother's right, kid. Bundy Street is kind of a slum. At least that's what

192

it's turning into. Nobody cares how it looks anymore."

"I care!" snapped Angie. "And so does my sister." She pointed across the street at Caro, who had made it to the end of the mission and was leaning against the edge of the building, resting in the shade. Angie began sweeping furiously again, raising dust and flies and stale bread crumbs.

"Hey! Wait a minute, kid. You don't need to get violent about it." Chico reached out and took the broom from her. Then he began to sweep with long, powerful strokes right down to the end of the street.

When he finished, he handed her the broom and unlocked the door to Chico's. "I suppose you want me to call the sanitation department and have them clean up that mess of debris you and your sister swept into the gutters," he said.

Angie thought it over. "They might not come for a long time. Don't you think it would be better if we swept it up and put it in your big trash bins out back?"

"We? Are you talking about you and me?"

Angie nodded. "And Caro."

Chico muttered something she couldn't hear and disappeared. But he came back a few minutes later with a stiff-bristled push broom and several empty boxes.

When the gutters were clean and the debris filled one of Chico's bins, she and Caro leaned weakly against his counter and watched him rub his hands with soap.

"You have to wash up before you cook food, you know. It's a state law." He filled two paper cups with water and put them on the counter. There were flies in here, too. Angie watched them buzz and swarm over the greasy grill like bees over honey.

Chico sighed. "They're not my fault," he insisted. "This place gets hot. You have to open the windows." Angie glanced at the open garbage bucket beside him. "OK! OK!" He put both hands out as if to stop her from looking at anything else. "I'll clean it all up. I promise. Do you want me to buy a new apron, too?"

Angie nodded. "Good idea."

"It would give this place a little class," added Caro.

Chico glared and shook his fist. "Git that kid outta here!" he threatened. Caro just laughed. She had been threatened by Chico before.

They walked slowly back to Flo's. Angie stopped off at the apartment to put the broom in the kitchen and a Band-Aid on a large blister in the center of her right hand.

Her mother was heating water for instant coffee. "Where did you get that blister?" she asked.

"Sweeping. I think Caro has one, too." Angie left the apartment before her mother could say anything else.

When she got to Flo's, she knew something had happened. Flo and Caro were standing in the kitchen of Maria's. Flo was holding a bunch of daisies wrapped in green paper with one hand, and was pointing frantically at the kitchen counter with the other.

"I must be losing my mind," she muttered. "I put them here. I know I did. A whole stack of fresh tortillas. I made them early this morning, and then I went over to Old Lu's to buy some flowers for the tables. When I came back just now, they were gone."

She slapped the flowers down on the sink and put both hands on her hips. "That does it. I've heard of rats stealing food before, but a whole stack of fresh tortillas is too much. That house next door is a disgrace. I'm calling the exterminators today. They can throw a tent over the top and fumigate the whole thing."

"But, Flo," Angie said, "I don't think rats even like tortillas."

"Hungry ones do. I don't want to hear anymore about it. That house is contaminated, and I'm going to see that something gets done about it."

Angie didn't say anymore. Flo was always upset about the house next door, and this was just a good excuse to have it taken care of.

But as soon as she got a chance, Angie went through Flo's place and checked the back door. It was standing open. Flo wasn't the kind of person to leave a door open. Angie stepped into a narrow alley that led right past the back side of the vacant house next door.

Just a few steps, and she was right next to the house. She could see why Flo was so upset about it. There was trash everywhere: old boxes and rags and even some furniture with the stuffing falling out. It was all pushed up against the house. If you wanted to get in from this side, you couldn't use the door. You would have to crawl in through a window. Probably that open one, with the chair propped up beneath it. She didn't want to go in, but she stood there a minute, looking and listening.

She heard the same sounds she always did: the cars on the street in front; the 10:05 bus, whooshing as it reached the corner; a siren, far in the distance. But all these sounds were the ones she heard every day. Unless she really thought about them, she hardly heard them at all. They were just the sounds of the city breathing.

It was something else that had made her stop and listen. It was unmistakable. Someone was coughing, and the sound was coming from inside the old house.

Angie knew who it was. She had heard Arnold Tooker's cough before. It made her want to put her hands over her ears and run. Instead, she stood there and remembered what Jessica had said: *Took's mother is looking for him.*

Involuntarily, Angie shook herself, like a wet dog shakes off water. *So what? Let her look.* Angie was the only person who knew where he was, and she didn't intend to tell. For all she cared, Took could sit in that old house until the rats ate him.

When she got back to Flo's, she went straight through the back door and shut it behind her. She stood there shivering, as though someone had been chasing her. She knew she was safe. She wasn't afraid of Took. So why couldn't she shake off the feeling that she still had to run?

By the end of that week, Angie could begin to see a change in Bundy Street. At first things had moved slowly. People had seemed a little embarrassed by the whole idea. Then they had become even more embarrassed by Angie and Caro sweeping their sidewalks for them. So they had brought out their own brooms. One thing had led to another. Now, the whole block looked cleaner, and it had begun to smell like soapy water and fresh paint.

The second week was the busiest. By then, no one had any excuse for not knowing what was going on. Chico saw to that. He was the best chain reactor Angie had ever seen. She and Caro had been good examples, but Chico was a persuader.

"Clean up your place, or move out," he said. Then he softened the threat with, "Come on in for a cup of coffee and see how my place looks."

Angie had to hand it to him. He kept his word. The open garbage can disappeared, and so did his ragged apron. He even sanded down the picnic table until it was smooth and covered it with a coat of green enamel. There were still a few flies, but they weren't big and they didn't buzz. At least now you could handle them with a flyswatter.

Pete painted white lines on his parking lot. He had a little paint left over, so he brushed a fresh coat on Old Lu's cart. Someone at the Oak Apartments got hold of a long hose and washed down the brick face of the building. Then they had to hose down that whole side of the street, because it looked as if it had rained mud. Angie thought that washing the building was quite an improvement. But she was really surprised when she went out one morning and saw that the black iron fire escape that zigzagged down the front of the building had been painted bright red.

When the owner of the Mayan Theater cleaned out the dust and debris from the entrance behind the ticket booth, he discovered that the whole thing was inlaid with pieces of mosaic tile. It had been covered with dirt for so many years that everyone had forgotten that it was originally blue and gold. When it was washed and polished, it caught the afternoon sun.

Everybody began to dump their cleaning water around the little trees that were planted in the sidewalk. Just as if there had been a summer rain, they sprouted new pale green growth and stood up straight and tall.

But their ugly wire cages bothered Angie, and she told Tony so. "They may be for protection," she said. "But they look like prisons, and they collect trash."

The sunbather was on his knees patching the last piece of broken plaster in front of the mission when she said it. The next morning all the wire cages up and down the street glowed with the same gold paint that covered George Washington. The funny thing was that when those wire cages stopped looking ugly, people stopped filling them with trash.

Corky was the only one who didn't really understand what was going on. He planted a chain-link fence around Customer Parking Only and put up a sign that said Keep Out! Angie laughed to herself when she saw it. She wondered what Corky would say if the fence was covered with morning glories next spring.

Flo polished the windows of Maria's until the green plants inside showed through the glass. Then she took a bucket of paint and covered the front doors of both her stores and all the window trim with a bright yellow color. She said Bundy Street was beginning to look like an old, wrinkled woman with a new spring hat.

But her idea caught on, and in a few days the doors up and down Bundy Street changed colors. Blue, green, red. Caro said they looked like welcome mats hanging in the air.

It was time for welcome mats. It was Wednesday. Tomorrow morning Con was coming home.

19
HOMECOMING

Con arrived about ten o'clock in the morning. Tony went to get him and brought him home in a taxi. Everyone on Bundy Street was crowded around in front of the Deli, waiting. Everyone but Angie and her mother and Caro. They were still busy inside, getting things ready for the party. The three of them had been helping Tony for two days. Early that morning Flo had appeared with enough hot tamales to feed fifty people. It was going to be more than a party. Bundy Street was having a real celebration.

When the taxi pulled up at the curb, Tony got out first. There was a hush, as if the whole block was holding its breath. Then Con appeared, his crutches first, and finally the rest of him, easing out of the cab, an inch at a time. Suddenly, his shoulders tensed, and he was standing, straight and tall, and smiling shyly, as if he had done something clever for the first time.

He got a surprised look on his face. "Hey," he said as he looked slowly up and down the street. "What happened around here, anyway? Everything looks different. It . . . looks great! Really great!"

Bundy Street let out its breath, breathed in again, and cheered. Everybody kept clapping and yelling while he walked slowly across the sidewalk and stood in the doorway of the Deli.

"I . . . want to thank everybody," he said. "You were all really good to me when . . . I was sick." Then Con leaned one of his crutches against the wall and lifted one arm. It was like a kind of salute. It said, clearer than words, "I'm glad to be home."

Angie could only see his back from where she stood inside the store. But she saw that he held himself straight and tall. She was ashamed to think that she had wanted to keep him in a wheelchair. Then he turned, with both crutches under his arms, and saw her.

"Hi," he said softly.

"Hi, yourself," she whispered back.

For a second it seemed like they were the only two people in the room. Angie wondered how she could have forgotten that when Con was happy his eyes seemed full of sky.

Then there were people everywhere, talking to Con and patting him on the back and helping themselves to hot tamales and pastrami sandwiches. Con sat on a stool and talked to everybody. On the counter in front of him was Flo's vase with one single, fresh flower. Angie had brought it from the hospital the night before and filled it early this morning.

After a while Tony went to the back room and brought out a large sheet cake. It was chocolate inside and out, but the letters that said Welcome Home, Con, were as yellow as sunshine.

Con cut the cake himself, and passed the first piece to Angie. Tony put his arm around her shoulder, but she knew he was looking at her mother when he spoke.

"We're all together today," he said.

Con shook his head. "All but one." He looked around at the crowded room. "Does anybody know what happened to Took?"

A few people shrugged, but most of them just went on talking. Caro was the only one who answered. "You know Took. He won't show up unless he really wants to."

"I know." Con smiled at her. "But this is the first time I've known him to miss a party."

Angie put her cake down without tasting it. She hadn't eaten much all day, and she still wasn't hungry.

"What's the matter, Angie? You look funny." Caro edged up closer. "Aren't you going to eat your cake?"

Angie shook her head. "You eat it. I'm . . . I guess I'm too excited to eat." She turned to listen to Flo. She was telling the story of the missing tortillas.

"The whole stack was gone," Flo insisted. "A

202

stack of tortillas doesn't just walk off by itself."

Tony laughed. "Well, Flo, those rats you've been telling us about must be strong ones, because I missed a few things around here this week myself. One of them was half a gallon of milk. If a rat managed to carry that off, I'll . . ."

"I've been missing things, too." Chico had joined the group. "Listen, Flo. I think it's just some kid."

"Rats!" Flo insisted. "But you don't have to worry about them, because I know where they're coming from, and I've already taken care of it."

Everybody stopped talking and looked at her. She nodded vigorously. "I called the health department about that house, and they called the owner. It seems that he's trying to sell the place, but it has termites. The exterminators are coming early tomorrow morning. By the time they cover the place with plastic and spray poisonous gas inside, nothing that lives there will have a chance."

Angie swallowed. *Took lives there, Flo. I heard him cough. He's hiding inside that house.* But instead she said, "Good for you, Flo. It's about time someone cleaned the rats and bugs out of the neighborhood."

She picked up a paper cup full of punch and pretended to take a drink. Took would just have to find someplace else to hide. Nobody was making him stay in that old house anyway. In the morning when the exterminators came, he would hear them, and he'd get out.

But what if he didn't? What if he was asleep and

didn't wake up in time? What if he was sick? Angie tried to keep her mind from visualizing the plastic tent that would cover the old house. It would be sealed off. No air could get in. And then the gas would start pumping, filling the rooms like cold fog filled the streets.

It's none of my business! Arnold Tooker isn't my responsibility. Anyway, I didn't actually see him. I only heard somebody cough.

She had heard somebody cough all right, and there was no mistaking who it was.

Angie jumped when Con reached out and touched her hand. "Hey," he said and placed one finger on the tip of her nose. "How about it?"

She knew what he meant, and she forced herself to smile back at him. It was their old secret, their signal for a smile that said, "I'm OK ... you're OK."

But Angie wasn't OK. Her skin felt hot, and her throat was dry. The sight of all that food made her sick. It wasn't fair. She shouldn't have to think about Took. She wasn't his keeper.

But who was? Angie was the only person who realized what was going to happen if he didn't get out of that house before morning. Angie tightened her fists in anger and frustration.

For the rest of the day she concentrated on keeping Took out of her mind. She talked to Con, and worked at Flo's, and talked to Con some more. Then she went home to lie down and close her eyes, because her head ached, and she felt heavy and tired all over.

She lay in the apartment, pretending to sleep, while her mother got ready and left for work. Caro came by and looked at her a couple of times. Angie recognized her footsteps and knew that she was standing right next to her, looking at her to see whether she was really asleep or not. But Angie didn't move. She didn't want to talk to anybody or do anything. She just wanted to lie there with an empty head.

That was the trouble. Her head wouldn't stay empty. No matter how hard she tried, Angie couldn't stop thinking about tomorrow morning, and that meant she had to think about Took.

She opened her eyes and sat up. She felt terrible, and it was all his fault. He had no right to hide in that awful place or steal food or cough so that she could hear him. Besides that, he had ruined Con's homecoming. At least, he had ruined it for her. Well, he wasn't going to get away with it.

Angie stood up. She was going to the old house. She was going to climb through the back window and find Took and tell him about tomorrow morning. She also intended to tell him exactly what she thought of him. That ought to be enough to turn him into a missing person for good.

Angie smiled. She felt better already. Arnold Tooker wasn't going to be on her conscience. As soon as he left the old house, she would be rid of him forever. She went out the front door and tried not to think about the rats.

It was early evening on Bundy Street. The sky was still light, but the sun had dropped low behind the buildings of West Los Angeles, and long shadows darkened the sidewalks and cooled the warm July air. It was that time of day when every- thing seemed a little out of focus, as if someone had smudged all the sharp details with blue dust.

Angie walked quickly. She didn't want anyone to see where she was going. This was private business—between her and Took. She went all the way around the corner at Sixty-fourth Street and entered the alley at the back of the old house.

She walked as quietly as she could, but she wasn't sure why. People always walked quietly, she realized, when they weren't quite sure what they'd find.

But she found things just the way she had seen them two weeks ago. Boxes of trash and old furni- ture were still piled up against the house. Debris was still scattered on the ground. Except for a few pieces of paper shuffled by the wind, nothing had changed. At least, not on the outside.

Angie stopped and listened. She didn't hear any- thing from the inside, either. Maybe the house was deserted. Maybe Took had already gone. But that didn't help Angie. She had to know for sure.

She went to the side of the house next to Second Chance, where the chair was still propped under the open window. The chair only had three legs, but it had been turned against the wall so that it wouldn't fall over. When Angie tried it, it seemed to hold her weight. She put both hands on the windowsill and pulled herself up.

The opening was wide enough, but the window

was stuck tight, halfway open, so that she had to either go through headfirst on her stomach or sideways, one leg at a time. She decided she would rather meet a rat with her foot than with her face, and swung one leg over the sill, crouching low, so her head would miss the window. She felt for a foothold and found it. Then she eased herself into the room and stood, motionless, waiting for the pulse to stop pounding in her throat.

The house wasn't empty. It was full of dark shadows and shapes. Whoever had lived there had left a lot of stuff behind them. Mostly junk, like the broken bed in the corner and the box of books with the pages half eaten by rats. But there was a small table with four good legs. Angie moved forward cautiously. On the table was a candle, stuck in a pool of melted wax, a package of matches that said Maria's, and what looked like part of a sandwich. Angie poked at it with the back of one finger. It wasn't a sandwich at all. It was a piece of rolled-up tortilla, and it was as hard and dry as a stale crust of bread.

She heard something from another part of the house. A click. Like the sound of a door being carefully closed. Then she heard another sound. She couldn't be sure, because it seemed muffled and far away, but Angie thought someone was coughing.

She shivered and rubbed both arms with the palms of her hands. She must be out of her mind. How could she be so sure it was Took she had heard that day? Anyone could be hiding in a place like this. She was a fool to be in here alone; it was getting darker all the time.

"Took?" She called his name softly and tiptoed across the room to a door that opened onto a central hallway. "Took?" Her voice was almost a whisper.

Something furry brushed against the side of her foot and scurried across the floor. Two bright eyes shone against the darkness at the back of the hall. Angie could see the shape of its body and the curved tail that lay against the floor like a piece of long, thick elastic.

Angie shuddered and hugged herself. Horrible little creature. She tried to remember: Did rats bite? She was almost sure they did. She backed slowly along the wall until she came to another doorway on the opposite side of the hall. It was open, and she went in. Something rustled under a pile of papers in a corner, and then everything was still.

Angie couldn't see as well in here. A dark blind covered the only window, and almost no light came in from the hall. It reminded her of the darkness of Con's hospital room that first time she had gone to see him. Only there was something different about this place. No one was resting in here. And it was dirty. It smelled old and stale—and fearful.

"Took!" She said his name firmly. Her voice had a hollow sound in the empty room. She felt like she was speaking to the air. "Took, listen. It's me. Angie."

Nothing happened. Angie stood absolutely still and strained her ears to catch the slightest sound.

She listened so hard, she almost felt that she could hear the old house breathing. She did hear the sound of breathing! Heavy and strained, like it was being pumped through too small a hole. In and out, in and out. Then she heard the other sound. A painful, hacking cough that always ended with a wheeze and could belong to only one person.

"Took!" Angie said his name louder. "Took, I know you're here. I'm not leaving until I talk to you."

She walked across the room to the closet door and put her hand on the knob. This was what she had been waiting for. Took was on the other side of that door, and she was ready for him.

For an instant her mind zeroed in on his image. If it hadn't been for Took, Angie was sure all her dreams would still be intact. He was the reason for everything bad that had happened to her. She took a deep breath. Once Arnold Tooker was out of her life, Angie was sure she would be OK. She turned the knob and opened the door.

He sat huddled on the floor of the empty closet with his back curled into the corner and his legs doubled underneath him. One candle stood in a chipped dish on the floor. It was burning, and he kept holding his hands out over the flame as if he needed to warm them. Angie saw that his hands were shaking. So was the rest of him. His teeth made little clicking sounds when he tried to talk.

"Took," she whispered. "What's wrong?"

"Close the door!" He wheezed loudly, trying to get his breath, and made urgent beckoning motions with both hands. "Quick! Quick! Close it so they won't get in!"

They must be the rats. Angie remembered wishing once that the rats would get him. But now that she'd seen one, she wasn't sure she would wish that on anybody. Not even Took.

She slipped quickly into the closet and pulled the door shut behind her. It was awful in there. Took looked sick and smelled dirty, and the candle was one of those cheap scented ones that made you nauseated if you stood around smelling it very long.

As soon as the door was closed, he acted like he had forgotten anyone was there. He rested his head against the wall and rubbed his hands together over the candle. Then he began to cough. His face screwed up as if he were in pain, and he held one dirty hand around his throat and tried to get his breath.

Angie kept remembering that day at La Mirada Beach when he had climbed to the top of the gymnasium cage on the sand and shouted, "Look at me! I'm at the top!"

Well, he sure wasn't at the top now. He was right at the bottom where he belonged. Angie stood, looking down at him. She wondered why she didn't enjoy seeing him like this.

"Hey, Took." She reached over and touched him on the shoulder just like she had poked at the stale tortilla in the other room. "Hey, Took. I've got to tell you something."

He lifted his head slowly, and he looked at Angie

as if he had never seen her before. Caro had looked like that once when she was really sick and had a high fever. She had looked at Angie and her mother as if they were strangers, and she had said some things that didn't make much sense. Delirious. That's what her mother had called it, and that was what Took acted like right now. Angie wondered if he was going to understand anything she told him.

"Took. You've got to listen to me. This is really important. They're going to fumigate this place in the morning, and you have to get out."

Took lowered his head and began to cough. "Cold . . . " He shivered. "I'm awful cold."

Angie sighed. He was the most exasperating person she had ever known. She had gone to a lot of trouble, and he wasn't even listening.

"Took! Look at me. It's Angie."

"Angie?" He pulled back away from her as if someone had threatened him. His eyes weren't Took's eyes at all. The old sly look that had always made her want to look the other way was gone. He reminded Angie of a small, trapped animal that was too weak to fight.

"Don't hurt me," he whimpered. He put up one hand as if to keep her away. "I didn't mean it. Honest, Angie. I only wanted . . ." He began to cough. His eyes glazed and closed, and he shivered violently.

Angie shivered, too. He looked really sick. She got down on her knees and put one hand on his forehead. His skin was hot and dry. She couldn't believe how hot it was. He was making so much noise breathing that she could hardly catch his next words. She had to lean over next to him and put her head close to his.

"I . . . lied, Angie. Accident . . . my fault. Con . . . was . . . was trying to save . . . me." He took a deep breath and began to cry. There weren't any tears, just dry, racking sobs that filled his throat and made him cough harder. "I'm . . . sorry. I'm so sorry. I wish I was . . . dead."

Suddenly, he was silent. His eyes closed, and his coughing stopped, and the only sound in the closet was the sound of his strangled breathing. In and out, in and out.

The candle flickered. In a few moments it would go out. Angie closed her eyes and leaned her head against the wall. She thought how good it would feel to put her head on a pillow in her own bed with clean, cool sheets covering her. She would like to pull them all the way up over her head the way Caro always did.

But she wasn't at home. She was in a dark closet with Took. She felt all tight inside, just the way she had felt that night on the roof when she had asked for help and it hadn't come. It wasn't coming now, either.

If you're my father, why won't you show me what to do? Why are you always putting me behind a closed door and keeping me there?

Angie had never felt so frustrated in her life. It seemed like everything she had planned to do had drained out of her and left her empty inside. She looked at Took, huddled miserably in his dark corner. She couldn't leave him here. He had become her responsibility, whether she liked it or not.

She leaned over and felt his head again. He looked even worse than he had before. And his breathing sounded funny. It came in quick little gasps.

His eyes flicked open. ". . . scared, Angie. I'm so scared. Please . . . don't hurt me."

She pulled back as if she had been burned. But what he said was true, wasn't it? She had wanted to hurt him. He was obnoxious, dirty, rude. He lied and cheated, and she hated him. Now here she was, sitting with him on the floor. She was the only one who could save him. She remembered the night on the roof when he had seen a candle flicker in the window and wondered why it had taken her so long to find out what she had to do.

She reached out and touched his hand. "I won't hurt you, Took. I'm telling you the truth. Nobody's going to hurt you." Angie looked at him and was surprised. She saw a human being.

She took a deep breath. Even in the rancid air of the closet, it seemed to go all the way to her fingertips. She got up on her feet. The closet door was still closed, but it wasn't locked. She could open it and walk out whenever she was ready. But she had to bring Arnold Tooker out with her.

She pulled at his hand. "Come on, Took. Let's get out of here."

He wasn't much help. He was sick and weak, and

he was afraid of the rats. He mumbled and protested and kicked over the candle so that there wasn't any light at all. Angie had to fumble until she found the doorknob. It turned easily, and the door swung open.

She half dragged, half carried him into the hall. She knew she could never get him through that window at the back of the house. There was only one way out. She hooked Took's left arm over her shoulder and her right arm around his waist. He wasn't very heavy. She was surprised how easy it was to take him all the way to the front door. It was locked, but only from the inside. Angie slipped the bolt and turned the knob. But she had to pull hard to swing it open. It creaked protestingly. No one had tried to open it for a long time.

It was past twilight on Bundy Street. The streetlamp on the corner sent a ring of yellow light through the warm summer air. A golden ring, Angie thought, reaching out and wrapping around them both.

"Come on, Took. It's only a little further," she said. "I'm taking you home."

20
CATCH A GOLDEN RING

Angie's mother took one look at Took and got him to the hospital as fast as she could. Tony went with her in a taxi, and they were gone for a long time.

Angie and Con waited on the front porch of the apartment building. Caro was with them, but she was asleep, with her head in Angie's lap. Con leaned his crutches against the railing and eased himself onto the top step, and that's where he stayed. Angie was sure he was uncomfortable and tired after the long day. But he wouldn't budge until they found out about Took.

It was a hot night, but it was even hotter inside the buildings. People walked up and down Bundy Street, or leaned against the lampposts, or sat on the red fire escape of the Oak Apartments. Some of them brought out folding chairs and sat right on the sidewalk.

Except for the two streetlamps, it was dark. Voices floated on the air like muted instruments, all playing at the same time but without direction. An occasional match struck with a burst of fire that danced like a firefly, then disappeared.

Finally, after about two hours, they saw Tony and Angie's mother coming along the sidewalk. They were walking close together. The light of a passing car spotlighted them in its headlights, and Angie caught her breath.

"Look!" she said. "I think they're holding hands."

Con looked at her and laughed. "It's about time," was all he said.

Angie's mother looked a little flustered. Her cheeks were pink, and Angie didn't think it was because of the walk from the hospital. Tony looked fine. His shoulders were back, and his head was high. Angie thought he was walking as if he were eight feet tall.

"Took is going to be OK," he told them. "But it's a good thing Angie found him when she did. He has pneumonia, and he'll have to stay in the hospital for several days. That boy really did a pretty good job of hiding, didn't he? I guess he felt so guilty about Con's accident that he couldn't face anybody, not even his own mother."

Angie had forgotten all about Took's mother. "She's been looking for him," she said. "Jessica's the one who told me. She said that Took's mother is about ready to call the police." Then, as if to herself, "I didn't even know that Took had a mother.

But Jessica did. She must have talked to her."

Tony nodded. "She probably did. Jessica and Took are cousins, Angie."

Angie's mouth dropped open. "Cousins! You mean Jessica Smith is related to Took? I don't believe it."

Tony nodded again. "Sometimes," he told her, "it's a smaller world than we think it is." He stopped and frowned. "I don't know exactly where Old Lu lives, but she's always on her corner bright and early. I'll tell her about Took in the morning."

"Old Lu?" Angie and Con spoke at the same time.

"I guess not too many people know about that," Tony told them. "Took was always pretty much on his own, but Old Lu is his mother just the same. She's really not so old. But she has worked hard and stood out in the sun and the rain for so long that she looks older than she really is. I think she makes a pretty decent living selling her flowers, but she hasn't made much of a home for her son."

Angie looked at her own mother. She was young looking and pretty, and Angie loved her, even if she did want to send them to Aunt Martha's. "What's going to happen to Took now?" she asked. "After he gets out of the hospital, I mean."

"That's something else we'll have to think about later," Tony told her. "I understand the new owners of the old house on the corner are willing to rent it pretty cheap. It might make a nice flower shop."

Con was shaking his head back and forth. "I still can't believe it," he said. "Jessica is Took's cousin.

Do you know that in all the time I've known Took, he never once mentioned it? He never mentioned Old Lu either, but, now that I think about it, he used to hang around her corner a lot."

Angie nodded. "I noticed that, too. Once I saw her give him some money, but I thought she was just feeling sorry for him. What I don't understand is . . . how could his own mother let him disappear all this time and not do anything . . ."

She stopped suddenly, remembering how she herself had felt about Took. Could his mother have felt the same way? Is that how Jessica felt, too?

"Angie." Tony's voice was gentle. "You never know what's on the inside of another person. We all have our secrets." He yawned and put his arm gently around Angie's mother. "Right now, I think we had better call it a day." He helped Con to his feet and handed him his crutches, and they started off across the street.

Angie and her mother half carried Caro into the apartment and put her to bed. Then they stood a minute, just looking at each other. Angie was thinking about what she had seen a few minutes before: her mother and Tony, so happy together. And she remembered what Caro had said. "I'll bet she'd run if she could, but she's got us."

"Mom . . . about the other night. You know, when I heard you talking about Caro and me living with Aunt Martha? Well, I've been thinking. If you want us to go there, I guess we can stand it." Her stomach turned over, but she meant what she had said.

Her mother reached for her. "Oh, Angie, honey. I never mailed the letter. Tony was right. Families should be together. Anyway, I couldn't stand the thought of sending you girls away. I was just so worried about what might happen to you here." She looked thoughtful. "The last two weeks have been eye-openers, Angie. Bundy Street is changing."

Angie hugged her mother. Inside, she felt like a jigsaw puzzle that was finally being put back together again. A lot of the picture was still missing, but at least all the pieces were on the table.

Then her mother pulled away a little, and Angie saw that her face was pink, just like it had been outside. "I . . . have something important to tell you, Angie. Tony and I . . . That is, you do like Tony, don't you, Angie?"

Angie laughed out loud. She laughed so loud that Caro opened her eyes and sat up in the bed.

Like Tony? Tony was so special, she didn't even have the right words to tell how she felt. But she did the best she could. "After Con," she told her mother, "Tony Genovese is my best friend."

"Then you won't mind if he's your stepfather? If we all live at the Deli together? There's plenty of room in the back. I'm sure we can . . ."

Angie didn't even let her finish. "You and Tony and Con and Caro and me . . . and Bandit, too? We'll be the mixed-up family of Bundy Street!"

Caro lay back in the bed and closed her eyes. But she only pulled the covers up as far as her chin.

Angie had trouble sleeping that night. So much

had happened. It all seemed to be floating around in her head like a giant traffic jam. When she closed her eyes and tried to sort out the confusion of details, they made a kind of picture in her mind, and it always looked like . . . Bundy Street.

Finally, when it was almost daylight, she unlocked the apartment door, slipped the key into her pocket, and quietly went outside and stood on the front porch.

Bundy Street was quiet now, as if it were resting. In a little while, the sun would come up, and cars would move noisily along the street. Old Lu would take her place on the corner. Chico would sweep away yesterday's crumbs. Flo would plug in the big pot of coffee and start frying fresh tortillas on the hot grill. Con would open his eyes and know he was home.

A lot of it was the same, but at the same time everything was different. Bundy Street wasn't just a rundown block on the city's west side. It was made of people. They could laugh, and they could cry, and Angie knew now that they could care about each other.

Bundy Street would always be a part of her life. She knew it, and she didn't mind anymore. Because the sign over the mission was true after all. Prayer did change things. When you talked to God, he showed you how to grow. He was just like a father, leading you and guiding you and loving you, even when you were wrong.

That's exactly what had happened to her. God had led her like a father would, letting her know, down inside, what it was she had to do. It had started back on the roof when she had asked for help and didn't know it was already starting to come. He had shown her a light flickering in the old house. He had led her straight to Took. He had shown her how to unlock the door for another human being. He had spoken to her in feelings instead of words. Even when she had tried to turn and run the other way, he had led her, pointed her, prodded her, until finally she had to look her enemy in the face. And it wasn't Took at all. It was the bad feeling about him that lived inside of her.

She raised her eyes to the eastern sky, all blue and purple and pink and yellow. A shaft of sunlight thrust upwards and dazzled her from behind a cloud. The sun came up every morning, Angie thought, and it went down again every night. It was something you could depend on.

Tony called it opportunity. Mr. Erickson called it faith. But Angie knew what it really was. A promise. It was the future, all wrapped up in golden ribbon. God's gift to his children.

The brightness grew, pierced the early morning clouds, and pointed straight toward Bundy Street. Saturday's trash cans gleamed, and the windowpanes turned to white fire. Then the light spread.

Angie saw the climbing vine that she had called a weed. It was covered with blue flowers, opening wide and spreading their faces toward the rising sun—just as if they had been waiting to catch a golden ring of light.

Catching a golden ring, Angie thought, was seeing a morning glory grow out of a crack in the sidewalk and bloom. It was listening to Tony Genovese's gypsy music and feeling like a whisper on the wind. It was starting a chain reaction from one end of Bundy Street to the other. It was forgiving and being forgiven, understanding and being understood.

But just because you help somebody, just because you feel a responsibility, doesn't mean you own them. You have to let the people you love go free. Angie supposed that was the way God felt, too. He let you make your own decisions. Otherwise, you'd be just like Bandit, with a rope around your neck.

She sat a little while in the new sunshine, listening to the growing sounds of the day, and she thought that golden rings were a little like the circles that form when you throw a stone into a pool of still water. They grow and grow. If there were enough of them, they would cover the world.

At last she got up and went into the house. She had a lot of plans to make. First, she was going to see Con, just so she could tell herself he was really home. Then she was going down the street to buy a flower for Took. She wondered what he would think when he saw her coming to his hospital room, carrying a flower from his mother's cart.

In the afternoon, she was going to keep a promise she had made a long time ago. This was the day she was going to take Caro to La Mirada Beach.

She remembered how she'd felt that time with Con when she had ridden on the carousel for the first time. She had been kind of afraid to try. But she had taken a chance, leaned out and stretched herself farther than she thought she could. She had touched the golden ring, felt it slip away, reached out again, and then she had finally held it in her hand.

She held it now. But not in her hand. It was deep inside her, like a warm glow. She smiled to herself. She could imagine what Caro would say when she saw the merry-go-round.

"I can't catch the golden ring, Angie. My arms are too short."

But Angie would help her. She would have lots of time to show Caro that you don't have to have long arms to catch a golden ring. You reach out for it with your heart.

Leave Beedee . . . Never!

Good-bye, Beedee
Marcia Stallings is a horse lover. But Dad says they
hav͟ ͟ ͟ ͟t͟h͟e͟ ͟r͟a͟n͟c͟h͟ ͟a͟n͟d͟ ͟m͟o͟v͟e͟ ͟t͟o͟ ͟K͟a͟n͟s͟a͟s͟ ͟C͟i͟—
into a cramped, ugly ͟ ͟ ͟ ͟ ͟ ͟ ͟ ͟ ͟ ͟ ͟ ͟ ͟ ͟ ͟ ͟ ͟ ͟e's
marrying a woman who doesn't know anything about
horses! Dad says it's all for the best, but how can it
be?

Once Over Lightly
Marcia's life is just about perfect. A job at Gatlin
Stables and a chance to compete in horse shows are
dreams come true. Then Marcia meets handsome
Barry Warwick, and life isn't so perfect anymore.
Why does he take an instant dislike to her? Could he
be the one sabotaging her work?

Oklahoma Summer
A whole summer back on her grandparents' ranch!
But things have changed. The work is hard, the
weather's hot, and Marcia doesn't trust Lester, the
ranch hand, who seems to hate horses. Even her old
friends have changed. Then Barry Warwick arrives
and Marcia's summer has a different look. . . .

NORMA JEAN LUTZ, author of the Marcia
Stallings books, is a free-lance writer. She lives in
Tulsa, Oklahoma.

Chariot Books
David C. Cook Publishing Co.